THE HIDDEN PLACE

THE
HIDDEN
PLACE

By PEERY SMITH

NEW YORK, E. P. DUTTON & CO., INC., 1962

E426194

AUTHOR'S NOTE:

William Deakens' journal is based on an
actual journal in the library of the Oregon
Historical Society.

Library of Congress Catalog Card Number: 62-7834

TO PETER

THE HIDDEN PLACE

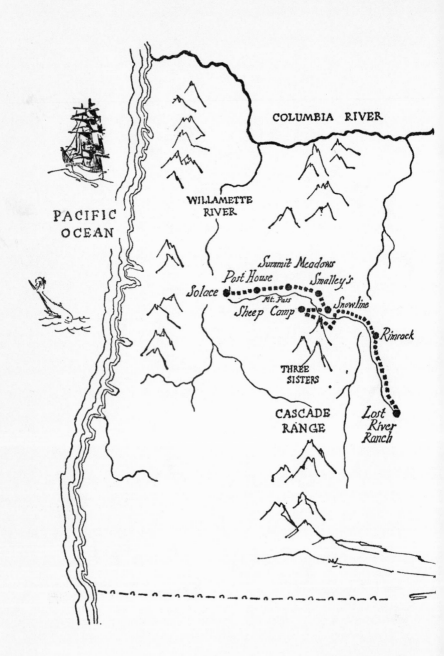

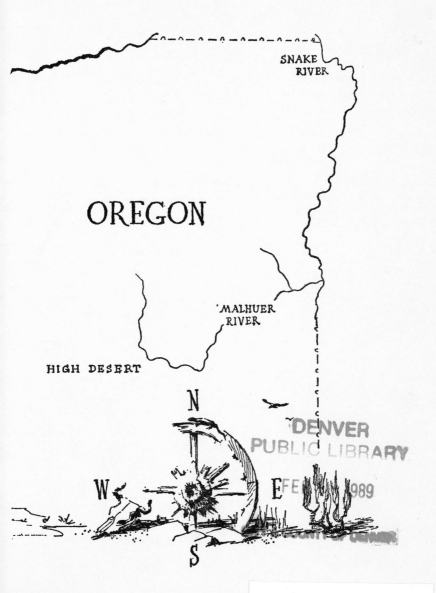

OREGON

SNAKE
RIVER

MALHUER
RIVER

HIGH DESERT

N

W   E

S

CHAPTER 1

HE CAME RIDING UP to our front door on Shone, my father's Appaloosa, and that was my first glimpse of Reece Morley.

I knew by Shone's heaving sides and frothed mouth that something was amiss, but it was my sister Chelly who got to the rider first. She went flying past me before I could free myself of the harness I was mending.

Chelly, who was sixteen that spring of 1882, had just put on long skirts and pinned up her hair. Now it was blown in disorder about her pretty face, and I could see by the look the stranger gave her that his reason for being there was momentarily forgotten.

A high-stepper, I thought to myself, noting with the disdain of a fifteen-year-old the tight, striped pants tucked into polished boots and the buttoned coat not made for easy riding. Here in the Oregon country a man had little use for a coat except for winter warmth. The rider had bold eyes and a smallish mouth, and when he lifted his dust-colored Stetson his light hair shone bright as new tin in the morning sun.

I hurried off the porch and pushed ahead of Chelly who was standing before the stranger at the stepping block.

"What's happened? Where's Father?" I asked. We had been watching the mountain pass all week hoping for the dust cloud that would announce his return with the cattle. I reached for Shone's bridle, resenting the possessive way in which the stranger held my father's cherished horse; but he jerked the rein quickly away from my hand. It was then I saw that the rifle he held so lightly was Father's Winchester.

He swung down out of the saddle, easy on his soft boots, his arm cradling the gun, and introduced himself more to Chelly than to me. He was still keeping a tight hold on Shone's bridle reins.

Trumpet, the hound, set up such a baying that it brought Aunt Marth hurrying to the front door. At sight of the stranger with Shone, she came marching down the stoop, straight and commanding as a general, which was her way.

"What's the matter?" she demanded.

Aunt Marth was a heavy-featured woman with shards of black still streaking her gray hair in spite of her seventy-odd years. Now she held her shoulders stiff as if braced against a blow.

Reece Morley gave her a quick look.

"I'm grieved to be the bearer of bad news, ma'm." He hesitated.

"Out with it, man," Aunt Marth said shortly. "Waiting won't change it. Has something happened to John?"

"It was an accident. He was cleaning his gun. He never knew what happened."

Father handling a gun carelessly! I couldn't believe it.

Chelly threw her apron over her head and burst into violent weeping. As for me, I could only stand there numb with misery, hating myself for the weakness of a fever that had kept me from being with Father on our yearly cattle drive.

"I'll have that gun, young man," Aunt Marth said harshly, coming directly up to him and reaching out a firm hand for it.

I thought Reece Morley hesitated a moment, as if unwilling to part with the rifle. When he handed it to her, she broke the barrel, lifted it to her nose and sniffed it with a curious intentness.

"When did this happen, and where are the cattle?"

You must not think my Great-aunt Marth a hard woman not to weep. I knew full well her deep abiding tenderness and the love she had for Father, but she was a pioneer woman who had faced the hardships of the Oregon Trail, Indian ambush and near starvation. She had suffered the tragedy of death too often to give way to it.

Reece Morley narrowed his strangely light eyes, either against the sun or in a closer measure of Aunt Marth, I could not tell which.

"We had driven off the road into Summit Meadow to rest and water the herd. John started to clean his gun . . ."

This meadow of natural grass high in the Cascade Mountains to the east was well-known to me. I could see my father, tall and stooped a little from fatigue as he must have been, sitting before the evening's campfire. I wanted to listen to no more, but I knew I must hear it through.

". . . There wasn't a cowhand to be hired when we started back from the rimrock country. A big drive into Ontario had cleaned them out. That is how I happened to join herds with John. He had picked up an Indian boy to trail-end us, but after the accident . . ." Reece Morley made a helpless motion with his hand. "I didn't know what to do. I couldn't trust the boy alone with the cattle until we were safely down on this side of the mountains where they could be corralled. All I could do was make the grave and bury John there."

"Put up the horse," Aunt Marth said, her voice strangely short of hospitality. "You'll need a fresh one to bring the cattle in.

"Chelly," she said, "come help me bring the mare in from

the pasture. We'll drive into Solace to Reverend Osburn. He'll want to toll the bell." She put her arms about Chelly's shoulders and drew her back into the house.

You must know that at this time my father, John Deakens, for whom I am named, was a cattle breeder living on the donation lands my grandfather, William Deakens, had settled here in the Willamette Valley in 1846.

Our farmhouse, a two-storied frame one, was built to the front of Grandfather's log cabin that now served as a kitchen and buttery. A row of locust trees shaded the narrow back porch that ran along the south side of the house from the sitting room to the kitchen. The trees hid from view the tombstones on Solace Cemetery hill, where lay the Deakens and my mother whom I could scarcely remember. Rail fences outlined our fields and orchards, and our well-cared-for barns and outbuildings showed with what pride my father held the place.

A mile and a half along the road to the north of us was the little town of Solace. In the time of the first settlers, Solace had been a trading post at the end of an old Indian trail leading from the bunch-grass country of eastern Oregon, through the Cascade Mountains into the lush green of the Willamette Valley.

It was the nearness of fine grazing for both summer and winter that decided Grandfather to halt his covered wagon on the banks of the Little South Fork.

Until the spring of which I am telling, I had expected to follow my father's way of life. The yearly cattle drives from the valley, over snow-capped mountains, through ancient lava beds, to the high desert plains where wild horses and cattle herds roamed, suited my love of excitement and adventure.

But that was before Reece Morley came riding to our door with the message of Father's death.

When I could come from hiding in the orchard with no tell-tale trace of weeping, I found Aunt Marth standing alone beside the buggy, waiting for Chelly. She wore her Sunday clothes with the dignity of a uniform; a jet-black bonnet, a black plush dolman, although the day was warm, and in her black-gloved hand she held her Bible.

"Will you burn Father's gun?" I managed to ask her. There is an old superstition in our country that a gun that has once killed will kill again, so such guns were always burned.

"No," she said. Then, seeing my questioning surprise, she added, "There's ample time for that, Johnny."

That evening Reverend Osburn sat with us while the church bells of Solace tolled out the forty years that were my father's age.

Reece Morley, when he had brought our cattle home, made himself so needed that he stayed. Barely a month later he married my sister Chelly against Aunt Marth's every known persuasion, his own being the greater. Seeing Chelly's love of gee-gaws and frippery, he showered her with such gifts—a gold neck chain and cross with big red and green stones, ear bobs, and lastly a sparkling ring too big for her small finger. But she wound it with wool and wore it, notwithstanding.

"If only I had sent her to Portland to study music, as your father wished," Aunt Marth moaned to me, her strong face breaking into furrows of pain.

"You are too young," she had pleaded with Chelly.

"You were married at fifteen," Chelly flung back at her, her childish mouth set in a new-found stubbornness.

But a tintype of Great-aunt Marth at sixteen showed a tall, handsome girl as she had looked at the time of the Indian War of '55. The old Henry rifle she had used in trying to defend her husband and child still hung behind her bedroom door. There had never been any of Chelly's flower-like prettiness about her. Only now she was helpless to defend our household against the stranger we had begun to fear, Aunt Marth and I, more than any Indian raider.

Little by little, Reece Morley, so mannerly and agreeable, began to shed his charms as easily as a snake sheds its skin. He seemed to have some hidden intention I could not fathom. But I could sense it, and I was young and defenseless against it. Once he had securely entrenched himself in the family, his manner toward Chelly became as authoritative as if he were dealing with a child, which, God forgive us, she was. Not that he was abusive. But when Chelly went secretly into Solace and had her picture taken wearing the necklace and ear bobs, and with her hand on her bosom to show her ring, and gave it to her husband as a surprise, he went into a temper and tore the picture to bits. He forbade her having any more taken. He said she looked like a silly dance-hall girl in all her finery. Then he took the jewelry from her and put it in a chamois bag he kept in his vest pocket.

As for me, he either ignored me or was openly contemptuous, and for some unknown reason I felt that he was trying to provoke me to quarrel.

It would have been an easy thing to do but for Aunt Marth's restraining hand. The trouble between us began with Shone. My new brother-in-law claimed to have traded six head of young beef cattle to Father for Shone, and refused to turn the stallion over to me. I did not believe him, but I had no way of proving him wrong, for the young steers were with the cattle the Indian boy, Billy Black Crow, brought home to us.

All this time Reece Morley was grazing and fattening his beef cattle on our lands, lands that by Father's death became half Chelly's—and he was Chelly's husband.

One day at breakfast he tripped the trigger of my temper to the firing point, bringing matters to a head. He had come to the table with his coat on and his boots strong with the smell of fresh polish, a habit I scorned, thinking him a dude for such vanity.

Aunt Marth had just lifted a side of browned spareribs onto the platter to carve. I was anticipating a second helping, for I had an insatiable appetite as a result of the fever, and was reaching for the pitcher of yellow cream for my coffee, when Reece pushed back his plate.

He watched me, his pale eyes bright as pebbles under water.

"Since you're too sickly to do any work around here, maybe you can stop eating long enough to ride Stumper into town and have him shod. I'll be needing a work horse tomorrow."

I could only stare at him, my mouth slack with astonishment.

Chelly dropped her head and giggled nervously.

The horse, Stumper, was a trusty old white cayuse who had lost his tail to a cougar, all except a stump just sufficient to hold a crupper. We had ridden his sway back as little children, but Father had long since turned him out to pasture with no thought of ever working him again.

Aunt Marth's hand stopped above the spareribs she was carving.

"We don't work Stumper." I strangled, red in the face, picturing the ridiculous figure I would make riding the old horse into Solace to the amusement of the boys along the street. I thought I knew now why Billy Crow had been sent on an errand on my pinto, leaving me no horse by which to lead Stumper. It was true that I was strong enough to ride again, although I had not done so up to now. There was Shone, of course, but other than Shone and the pinto, Reece had managed to sell the rest of our horses on one pretext or another.

"We?" Reece looked at me. "Oh, I wouldn't think of asking you to do any work yet, Sonny. I've got a man to do that."

The name "Sonny" infuriated me, as he knew it did, with its connotation of youthfulness which I was far from deserving.

"Stumper is too old to work." I could feel the blood swell my throat and face as I jerked back in my chair. My appetite was gone. The insolent smile on Reece's face drove me beyond discretion. "Besides, he doesn't belong to you." I could no longer contain myself. "He doesn't belong to you any more than Shone or anything else around here does," I yelled out in my passion. In spite of Aunt Marth's warning command to sit down, I was half up and out of my chair shouting my pent-up fury at him. I couldn't stop.

"My father wouldn't have traded Shone for any old steers. He wouldn't have sold Shone to you either. Someday I'll find out how you got him. Someday . . ."

Reece Morley slid toward me from his chair like a weasel to its prey. I made a grab for the knife in Aunt Marth's hand, but he was too quick for me. He had me by the front of my shirt collar in a strangling hold, and although I was a lithe enough boy, I was still weak and reedy from the fever and he was a man and stronger.

He half-pushed, half-dragged me across the dining-room floor through the door to the long back porch. I saw him reach for a thing I had never before seen around our place. It was a blacksnake whip coiled on the hatrack beside the door. I knew then that he had provoked this moment to use the whip.

I tried to twist away from him, but he pinned me to the wall, his knees bent hard against my writhing body. Even if he had freed me it would have been folly to run, for he could have cut my legs to slices with such a whip. I had seen Big Wes, the teamster, cut off the head of a rattlesnake from the lofty seat of his wagon, laying out the leaded tip of his whip with the explosive crack and sureness of a bullet.

Behind me I heard Chelly crying. Then Aunt Marth's solid tread hurried across the bare boards of the kitchen, retreating, I thought, beyond the sound of my beating.

CHAPTER 2

HE STOOD HOLDING ME there against the wall, enjoying my helplessness. A lark called clear and high over the clover field beyond in flight.

The kitchen door banged open.

"Mr. Morley!" Aunt Marth's voice from the doorway cracked with a lash of authority. "Take your hands off that boy."

She came a step out on the porch, holding by the handle the big copper kettle kept boiling for the dishes.

Reece Morley's face went blank with amazement. What he saw in Aunt Marth's black eyes and hard-set jaw left no doubt as to her intentions. His hand slackened on my collar, and I gasped with a painful intake of breath.

"And drop that whip, Mr. Morley," Aunt Marth ordered, never taking her unwavering gaze from him. "Johnny, pick that thing up and take it to my room; and when you do, stay there.

"This has always been a house of peace, Mr. Morley. We'll have no more quarrelling or fighting."

Reece Morley shifted his stance for a half-bow of mocking deference, as I picked up the whip and edged for the door behind me. But when he spoke, his words held no apologies.

"No man is going to let a mouthy young'un call him a thief

to his face and take it. He needs to mind his manners. He's been woman-pampered too long. His father would have done the same in my place."

"His father would have had no cause to," Aunt Marth said, lowering the kettle.

With a shrug he turned on his heels and went off the porch to the corral. Only then did I see Aunt Marth's mottled hands quiver and her shoulders sag as if her present burden was heavier than the kettle she was holding.

"Father would never have sold or traded Shone, you know that, Aunt Marth," I burst out, coming back to her ashamed and apologetic for my uncontrolled temper that had forced her to such a stand. "He wouldn't have let Chelly marry a man we don't know anything about either. Reece Morley is a thief. He's already sold our horses and everything he can lay his hands to. He won't stop, Aunt Marth, you know he won't."

Aunt Marth eased the kettle of boiling water to the porch.

"It's time I got the legal rights of this straightened out, Johnny. You're not of age, and someone must have the say of things around here. You see now the need for such learning as your grandfather had, and how it would stand us in good stead to have some knowledge of the law."

A great high secretary in our front parlor was filled with my grandfather's well-thumbed lawbooks, and it was my Aunt Marth's fondest hope that I would follow in his footsteps and become a respected member of Congress, if not a governor, as Grandfather had been in territorial times.

"I'll go into Solace and see what Luke has to say, 'though I've little respect for the man."

Luke Stover was a watery-eyed old man, a self-styled lawyer who gave more time to his bottles than his books, I'd heard it said. He had just enough knowledge of the law to make it serve his needs when it was to his own advantage. I could see little help from him against such a man as Reece Morley.

"But, Aunt Marth," I pointed out, "we've got no buggy horse." The one the family used was Chelly's, or so she liked to claim, and Reece had sold it as unfit. We knew by now that it was only a means of isolating us from Solace.

Aunt Marth took off her checkered kitchen apron and rolled it in her hand. "I walked most of the way from Missouri to Oregon, Johnny Deakens. I guess I'm still good for another mile or two. Likewise, there's a matter I want to talk over with Big Wes before he gets his freighter out of town."

Big Wes Hurnden drove an eight-horse team across the Santiam Pass from spring to fall. He brought in wool and hides and took back staples as were needed for the isolated ranch houses and cattle towns of the eastern Oregon country. He had driven past our place only a few days before and must return the same way. Trumpet always heralded his approach with a wail that ended in a far-flung bay. Since we could not possibly have missed the freighter, I wondered why Aunt Marth wanted to see Big Wes in Solace.

"I've a mind to speak to him alone and unheard," Aunt Marth explained, as if reading my mind. "There's a thing that bothers me, Johnny. I got no cause to stir up trouble if I'm wrong. If only I were a younger woman I'd ride the Pass and find out myself, but I can't leave Chelly, not now . . ." She stood a moment lost in frowning thought.

"You'd better finish your breakfast," she said abruptly, "then Chelly can wash up."

But for once I had no appetite.

Down at the corral Reece had mounted Shone and was spurring him onto the road just as Billy Crow rode up to the gate on the pinto. Suddenly, the pony lunged as if he had been raked with a spur in passing, throwing the Indian boy against the gatepost. I cried out and would have run to him, when he righted himself and rode stoically on into the barn without a backward glance at Reece, who jerked Shone's mouth viciously, wheeling him into a run toward Solace.

Aunt Marth watched his trail. "Their feet run to evil and they make haste," she quoted bitterly. She took up the kettle and turned for the kitchen. "Johnny, I want you to go up to my room and latch the door from the inside." Aunt Marth's room was the only one in the house that boasted a lock. "I don't trust your temper if he sets on you again. You promise to stay there until I get back, you hear?" And I promised.

It was a promise I had begun to regret almost at once, as my aunt's crowded room held little of interest. It was a long room to the back of the house with one window that opened onto the porch roof. A massive low-poster bed with a feather tick filled one end of it and a rag-carpet loom the other. The bang-bang of Aunt Marth's foot on the treadle was as usual a sound in our house as the tick of the Seth Thomas clock on the downstairs mantel. No scrap of worn or useless cloth but was stripped and sewn and rolled into balls to be woven into hit-and-miss carpets for our floors. The carpet loom was no novelty to me. I looked anxiously about for something to read, but other than Aunt Marth's Bible, there was nothing.

It was thus, prowling about, that I spied the newspaper with which the little open closet had been thriftily papered. The assassination of President James A. Garfield, in bold head-lines, interested me not nearly so much as the report of a bear hunt near Solace. I was at the point of the bear's attack when my reading matter was blocked by an overlapping sheet. It was easy enough to slip my pocketknife blade between the two pages where the flour paste had not held too tightly. But instead of the blade sliding down smoothly, the point struck metal and stuck. When I ran my hand over the spot to find the cause, I could feel the outline of a metal strip and the buried heads of the screws that held it. A funny thing, I thought, to be on a closet wall. I scraped the paper away to satisfy my curiosity.

It was a door hinge—a small hand-wrought hinge—one of two I found sunk in the planking of a small door. It took only a minute to slit the paper around the outline of the door and force it open on its rusty hinges.

What it opened onto was the attic above our kitchen, the log-cabin part of our house, at one time reached by an open stair, now sealed away and forgotten.

Peering into the gloomy cobwebbed depth of the attic space, I could see that it was a repository for all the discards of our house. I made out a broken cowhide-bottomed chair, a metal-bound trunk, and a spinning wheel. There was an easel on which rested a half-finished painting which I knew to be my mother's, for our front parlor held many bright pictures she had painted. But the thing that caught and held my eye was an ancient rifle on a tree-limb bracket, a powder horn, and a pair of saddlebags, cracked and blackened with age. Taking off my boots, I slipped cautiously across the puncheon floor. Below me, Chelly was putting the dishes away, and I did not want her calling up to question me.

I brought out the gun first. It was an old Kentucky rifle, a flintlock with a tiger-maple stock, and on its silver mounting was etched the name, William Deakens, and the date, 1844. It was my Grandfather Deakens' gun, the one he had carried from St. Joe, Missouri, across the plains to the Oregon Territory. I handled it with a curious feeling of excitement.

My grandfather, a literate man with a fondness for records, had kept a journal of his crossing, Aunt Marth had told me.

It was the remains of this journal that I came upon in one pocket of the saddlebag. The pages were torn and water-stained, the first part missing, the back leaves covered with accounts of later cattle buyings and sellings. I opened it midway to where the thin spidery writing was most legible. The heading of this page was: August 24, 1845. Hot Springs near Fort Boise.

"Five months since we left St. Joe," I read. "All heartily sick of the rigors of the trail and there is much dread of what lies ahead. There is great uncertainty as to the choice of the route from here on. We have met with a mountain man, Dan Bold, who claims he knows a route to cut two hundred miles from the regular Oregon Trail and eliminate many hardships. He offers to guide us for $5.00 a wagon and I am inclined to the offer since the agent here thinks him reliable. Two hundred families are of the same mind."

Further dates marked only condition of weather, food, and cattle, with here and there a sense of growing apprehension that all was not well.

". . . We are in the foothills of the Malheur Mountains. This name given by Peter Skene Ogden, a trapper of the Hudson's Bay Co., means 'Evil Hour,' from his having lost all his supplies and furs to the Indians at this spot. It is aptly called. All signs of the old trail we were to follow seem to have disappeared. The water is bad and many are sick with mountain fever.

". . . The cattle are restless and trying to take the

back track. Many of the oxen have lain down and refuse to get up."

The next entry was undated.

". . . We have reached a small stream, no doubt a tributary of the Malheur. We have come to an ordeal of boulders so thick that they hide the ground. Wagons are breaking to pieces. The hoofs of horses and cattle are being pounded to a bloody pulp.

"September 5. We have left the boulder country and have come down to alkali plains north and east of Malheur Lake. The water here is poisonous and Bold now admits we are lost. We must keep going or all will die.

"September 11. We have come to a Stinking Hollows. Even this bad water is of short ration and grass for animals is scarce. Everyone who can ride is out scouting for water. There is talk of lynching this man, Bold. I like this not for, as I have pointed out, this mountain man is the only one who is likely to get us through to The Dalles.

". . . Still no water. I returned this night to find the tongues of three wagons bound together and pointing upward ready for Bold's lynching. I have quelled these hotheads with threats of the law to follow and they have given Bold a reprieve of three days to find water."

This was a part of our family's adventure I had not heard. Excited by the discovery, I moved over to the window for better light.

"Bold has just come in with news of a spring some thirty miles to the north. It is midafternoon and we must march all night to reach it by tomorrow. Bold now seems sure of the way.

"Bold has come to me with as strange a tale as I have ever heard. He tells me that there is a small tribe of Indians at the headwaters of a crooked river lying to the south and west, which is a tributary of the Deschutes River we are soon to reach. He says he was there a year ago on a trapping expedition and that on following a deep and hidden canyon, he had come upon a spring of water in which chunks of gold could be picked up at ease. He says there is no end of it and that he had picked up enough to fill his saddlebags when he was set upon by the Indians, his horse shot out from under him and he escaped with nothing but his life. He tells me this out of gratitude for having saved him from the lynching and he trusts me to keep this secret. When we have reached our destination, he is of a mind to have me join him for another venture into this place of gold. He tells me that the Indians use these nuggets for ornaments and look upon them as having some protective magic power; and that they guard the place well, but that in the late fall of the year when they bring their horses down out of the mountains into the bunch-grass country, the place will be safe to be gotten to. He has marked this hidden place on a map which is meaningless to me, knowing nothing of this vast and ominous desert country other than in the passing.

"I have put the map here between these pages, well-concealed against the greed of some heedless man, but I have told Bold that I am only concerned with getting my family to the security of the Willamette Valley."

Here I found several leaves of the journal stuck together. When I freed them with my knife blade, I found a map that had been drawn on a page torn from the journal. It was not yellowed or aged as one might think, having lain here so long a time, although well-protected as I could see.

I had been sitting on the floor beneath the window while reading the journal. Now I jumped to my feet, a surge of excitement sending a rush of blood to my head.

In my mind's eye I could see the glitter of the gold in this hidden place. I could see myself gathering it up in handfuls to fill my saddlebags as Bold, the mountain man, had done. I thought of our present predicament, with Father gone and Reece Morley entrenched in our house, selling off our cattle; and that there was little chance that I should be able to build back the fine Durham herd or ride the Pass again. But gold would make me free of Reece Morley, and I could buy and build as I wanted.

In that moment I could see myself a man of importance with a spread as vast as Pete French, the cattle king, down on the California border.

The slipping sound of footfalls coming up the stairway jerked me back to a quick awareness of time and place. There was only one person who would be treading our stairs like that.

Grabbing up my boots, I pulled them on, my hands damp with perspiration as I tugged at the lacings.

The lock on Aunt Marth's door was a crude affair with a wooden hasp that fell into a hewn-oak slot screwed to the wall studding; but it was strong, and I did not see how Reece could open it without breaking in the door. I never doubted but that it was my brother-in-law who was coming up the stairs, and that he meant to have his way with me, knowing Aunt Marth was not there to interfere.

I waited for him to call out to me and order me outside, but he did no such thing. Then I saw the thrust of a narrow saw blade between the cracks of the door above the hasp, and I knew what he was up to. He would not have to break in the door. He had only to saw the hasp in two.

I looked frantically about for something with which to break the saw blade, but I knew it would be a losing battle for the hasp would break easily enough against his strength.

It was now summertime, and Aunt Marth's window was open, propped the height of the sash by a length of stovewood. The porch roof was below it, the butt of the locust tree pressing its edges. This was no new route for me, but never before had I followed it so swiftly or so silently.

I hit the ground on the run and made for the thicket of currant bushes that hedged the back yard from the orchard. I did not stop for breath but plunged ahead through the orchard and up the wooded hill toward the cemetery.

Scrub oak hid my climb over the rail fence into the high rank grass. Here I threw myself full length, panting and spent. Beyond me the marble shaft that marked my grandfather's grave stood like an outpost sentinel as if to guard me. High above me, the wind caught in the fir trees on the hilltop and set them to a melancholy sighing. What could I do? Where could I go? If, under cover of darkness, I went into Solace, I would still be at my brother-in-law's mercy. I did not trust Stover, the lawyer, to see me protected by law.

The road ahead leading over the Pass was not a walking road. I had no horse and could not go back for the pinto. Shone would have come to me at the soft whistle Father had taught me, but Reece knew this and kept the horse behind the bars of the corral.

It was the sound of the bells, the freight bells of Big Wes' eight-horse team, that decided me on my course. It was as if Father had reached down a hand from Heaven to point the way. I would hide in the freighter as it passed. Although Big Wes was a good friend of Father's, I was afraid he might stop me from leaving home. But once safely across the mountains and into the range lands, I was sure I could find work with the cattlemen.

By this time Trumpet was baying at the bells that slowed and ceased before our gate. Aunt Marth must have ridden home with Big Wes. However, I knew he must stop again here on the hilltop to rest the horses from the long, steep pull.

I slid through the grass to where the road had been cut away to lessen the grade, leaving a high bank thick with sweetbrier and honeysuckle. My hair, newly curled to my head from fever, caught in the briers, making the going painfully hard on hands and face. When I flattened myself on the rim of the bank, I found I would be on a level with the bed of the freight wagon as it passed.

Below me the bells again took up the jangling song. Soon I could hear the clop-clop of the horses' hoofs in the dust and their gusty blowing at the climb. Then, all at once, they were directly beneath me—Big Wes with his wide leather belt cinched like a surcingle about his quaking belly to steady it from the jolting of the wagon. His wide-brimmed hat was pushed back from his face, round and weathered as an oak gall, and he was singing. The words were lost to me, but his voice was high and sweet as a woman's, sounding strange to be coming from so heavy a man as Big Wes. He stopped abruptly with a "Whoa, there," followed by the screech and grind of the brakes.

Before the horses had quite come to their halt, I dropped from the bank to the tailboard of the freighter and squirmed under the high-ribbed canvas covering where I sprawled, trembling and dry-mouthed.

When I had gotten my breath, I started to sit upright, only to find that I was wedged in under a sewing machine and that kegs, wooden washtubs, and bundles of upright brooms crowded the space behind.

Just as I was maneuvering to a more comfortable position, Big Wes cracked the blacksnake. The freighter jerked forward, my head went back with the unexpectedness of it, and at that moment a man's hand reached out from behind to grasp my shoulder, pinning my back to the tubs like a hide on a wall.

CHAPTER 3

THE WARNING HISS for silence was so close I could feel the warmth of the man's breath on my cheek and the smell of him was suddenly strong in my nose.

"Black Crow see you run. Here no good place, Black Crow go too."

It was Billy Crow! I went limp with relief against the wheel of the sewing machine and sent it turning with a bang into the stack of upturned washtubs. But the renewed grinding of the wagon wheels, the clatter of the horses' hoofs, and the singing of the bells were enough to drown the noise from Big Wes' ears.

"How did you get here?" I gasped. When I turned my head, I could see in the dim light that filtered through the canvas that he had wedged himself behind the stacks of brooms flanking the sewing machine. "Where are you going, Billy Crow?"

"Way far. Big Belly go in house for talk. White Hair hide in barn for read book." There was silent laughter in his soft guttural words. I knew he meant that Big Wes had gone in the house with Aunt Marth and that Reece had made himself scarce at the time. It had been no problem then for Billy Crow to mount the wagon and stow away unseen.

The relief at finding that it was Billy Crow beside me was so great that it was some time before I realized that his presence was anything but harmless.

I had thought of showing myself once we were far enough

on the way that Big Wes would not turn me back. But now I could not do that without exposing Billy Crow as well. I wiped my damp face with my bandanna, wondering just what to do. Big Wes had no use for Indians, young or old.

Big Wes was an amiable man, blustering and noisy, with a speaking voice grown harsh from the steady stream of invectives he hurled at his horses. The words were purely habit and had no more sting in them than the forty-foot bull whip he cracked about the horses' ears to direct them from one side to the other around the narrow mountain curves. He had lost the two front fingers of his right hand in the Indian wars, so that handling a gun was not easy. Because of this, he had grown more skillful with his whip than anyone I had ever seen, and his exploits with it made for lively tales among the men in Solace.

For all his good nature, there was one subject that set him to unrepeatable words of violence: that was "Injuns." At defense of them, his big weather-burned face would congest to a dangerous purple, and the thin, revealing scar that welted the back of his hairline would stand out white as peeled willow, to point a reason for his hatred. Big Wes had been a scout in the Modoc Indian War of '73, and had trucked supplies to the army posts.

"A renegade he was, slipped up behind me out of a lava trench when I was belly-down at the lake for a drink with nary a horse whinny or a squawkin' jay to warn me. If it had been mules, now, I'd have known right off, for a mule can smell an Injun a mile away—stops 'em dead in their tracks. Thought he had me, but the bullet went through my arm and knocked me over a boulder.

"First pass he made at my scalp, I hove up and grabbed his greasy legs and squashed him with my gun butt flat as a sow bug under a board. Bunged up the hole in my arm with a siz-able cud of chewing tobacco, and helt my head under snow water to numb it. And I fetched that load of flour back to General Canby like I set out to do.

"There's one good thing come out of it, though: Never an Injun comes in a mile of me without I'm warned. Sets my scalp to crawlin'. 'Course, mostly I can smell 'em same as a mule does."

I had heard Big Wes repeat this to Aunt Marth soon after Reece Morley came to our place with Billy Crow trail-ending the cattle. Big Wes declared it was a thing my father would never have done, in spite of what Reece said. But I did not think that was so, for I knew Father's friendship for the In-dians. He talked to me often of how they had been cheated by the Indian agents and provoked to wars in defense of their lands. Father had sat in council and pleaded for Chief Winne-mucca when his people were going hungry, with the white hunters slaughtering elk and deer for the hides alone. It was Chief Winnemucca who had given Shone to Father in appre-ciation for his efforts.

As for me, I liked the silent-moving Indian boy with his black, banged hair, his deerskin shirt, and moccasined feet. I saw little of him, for he slept in the barn and ate at the stoop. Reece kept him at the cattle and sent him away the minute he was fed. But mornings when I went to sit on the kitchen porch in the sun, still weak from the fever, I would find in my chair a gift of thimbleberries, in a holder of maple leaves, their red cups still cold with dew. They grew on the damp and shady banks of the Little South Fork, as did the blackberries, wild lettuce, sorrel, and dock he must have thought I needed. Raven-ous from the fever, I ate them all, careful not to mention it to Aunt Marth.

All this I now thought of, wondering if Big Wes' scalp were crawling and what I should do if he decided to follow his nose to our hiding place.

But we jolted the endless dusty miles with no sign of discovery. From what I knew of the Pass road I was sure Big Wes would be stopping at the Soda Springs Posthouse overnight. My throat was parched for want of water and I was hungry. The appetite which the fever had left me seemed never to be satisfied.

Billy Crow slept like a doe in the sun. I could feel his quick alertness each time Big Wes stopped to rest and water the team, then the easy rhythm of his breathing to the singing of the bells. I wondered what Aunt Marth would think of my disappearance and if she would guess what had driven me to it. Would poor, frightened Chelly dare to tell her?

I must have dozed, for I was brought sharply awake by a man's voice yelling out to Big Wes to "pull in and hold up a spell," and I knew we were at the tollgate not too far from the Soda Springs.

"You got me my sewing machine, Wes?" It was Mrs. Turner, the talkative wife of the tollgate-keeper. I knew her well. "I declare, I can hardly wait."

And I was sitting on the foot treadle of the machine and no place to move!

"I shore have, Lizzie," Big Wes yelled out. "She's a Wheeler and Wilson, just like you ordered. Looks like George must have come onto the Lost Blue Bucket mine he's always prospecting for. Next thing you'll be having a parlor organ and store carpets."

I felt the grip of Billy Crow's lean hand on mine as he pulled me to the rim of the overturned tubs. I felt him lift the tubs behind me at the same time. With the instinct of a mole burrowing for its life, I slid headfirst under the tubs, twisting and squeezing my thin arms about me, making a ball of my body. My throat, dry from thirst and constricted with fright, gave me such a terrible desire to cough that I was forced to grip my nose and palm my mouth for silence.

How I prayed that Big Wes would deliver the sewing machine and hurry on, but Mrs. Turner had different plans.

I could hear Big Wes hefting himself down over the wheel with a grunt. "Thank you kindly, Lizzie, but I better push on. I'll be a mite behind as it is. Promised Aunt Marth I'd set a stone for John up on Summit Meadow in the morning. I was late in gettin' out of Solace with it. Haven't even stopped for a snack."

He was at the back of the wagon, unroping the canvas covering. "Better give me a hand here, George."

"That's a sorry thing about John Deakens," Mrs. Turner hurried to say, sounding anxious for any news Big Wes might give her. "But I guess the family was lucky he had that young fellow with him to bring the cattle in. He was mighty careful with them, too. George was over on Pot Handle Creek about that time, and he saw where the cows had been rested in Summit Meadow for several days. How's he making out down there, Wes?"

"He's makin' out," Big Wes growled. "He's makin' out real good. He's married the Deakens girl and he's settin' over the layout like a coyote over a kill. Beat Aunt Marth into Solace this morning and got hisself appointed young Johnny's gardeen. Told Luke Stover the boy drew a knife on him and tried to kill him. Says if there was any more trouble he'll have Johnny brought to law for attempted murder. Says he's gone loco from the fever and apt to kill someone if he's not watched. Talked as if he might even go further and have young Johnny put away in Salem. Luke drew up some legal-looking papers for Morley. Figure Morley must have influenced the law with some hard cash."

I could hear a venomous hiss of tobacco juice as it sprayed the dust on the wagon wheel.

Big Wes lifted the end of the canvas. I clutched myself in an agony of suspense, not daring to breathe.

"A fever can do queer things," George Turner agreed. "Had a nephew over in the John Day country had a mountain fever. Turned him silly as a sheep."

"Oh, poot! He was silly to begin with," Mrs. Turner snapped. "Johnny Deakens rode through here with his pa half a dozen times, and he didn't look mean to me. I've known lots of folks had typhoid and such, and all it ever done to their heads was molt off their hair. Come back in thick as a beaver pelt, as I recall."

The sewing machine was being lifted out. I could feel the scrape of it on the wagon bed.

"Washtubs!" Mrs. Turner exclaimed. "George, I've a mind to take one of those while I'm about it."

My ears caught the faint scuttle of Billy Crow's shifting body beyond the wall of upstanding brooms.

The tubs set level where they could be seen after removing the machine, and try as I would, I had not been able to draw in the toes of my boots. It was not that I feared Big Wes finding me so much as the Turners knowing my whereabouts. I knew Mrs. Turner was a lonely woman, eager for news and equally eager to pass it on. And what if the next man to come this way should be Reece Morley?

From what Big Wes had just been saying, I knew that Reece meant to be rid of me for good. As Chelly's husband, he would then have all the Deakens land.

If only I had been studiously inclined and less given to story reading, perhaps my grandfather's lawbooks would have given me some way of knowing whether Luke Stover's papers could send me to the asylum at Salem.

"No, Lizzie," I heard George Turner protest. "I took near an hour to drive the hoops down on that washtub of yours. It's tight as a drum and don't leak a drop."

"Then I'll be getting on," Big Wes boomed. "I'll just about make the Springs by lamplight."

The crack of his whip cannonballed the horses to action. The wagon gave such a violent lurch that I banged my head against the washtubs; my ears rang like a beaten pan, the gate clanged to behind us, and Big Wes sang out:

"Hi-ee, hup! Gee! Lay to, you spavin-legged, wind-suckin' old bag o' bones. Hi-ee, hup!"

Billy Crow lifted the stack of tubs and I crawled out, dizzy from the blow on my head, but more lightheaded from my good luck.

The sun had gone down, and now the cool of evening was beginning to creep between the rim of the wagon bed and the canvas. My blood was still thin from the fever, and the cool air set me shivering. I longed for one of the sheepskin coats Father and I always wore on our mountain drives. Big Wes began singing in his strangely thin, sweet voice, keeping a kind of rhythm to the bells.

> "Got a girl to the south, her name is Flo,
>   Ridin' high; ridin' low.
> Got a girl in the north, where I aim to go,
>   Ridin' high; ridin' low.
> Got a girl in the east; got a girl in the west,
>   Next girl I meet, I'll like the best,
>   Ridin' high; ridin' low."

I began thinking of warm blankets and hot food.

Of a sudden I felt Billy Crow's hand on my arm. Sliding from his shelter, his black head close to mine, he whispered his words of warning.

"Horse come fast. I think, no good."

I could hear nothing above the jolting of the wagon, Big Wes' singing and the jangling of the bells; but I knew an Indian's hearing was as strangely keen as a fox's and so I listened, straining for the sound.

Big Wes must also have heard the oncoming horse, for he stopped his singing and slowed the team to a drag. Now I could hear the hoofbeats coming up behind us at a gallop. But the sound of them was muted by the pounding in my ears, for I never doubted who it would be coming after us at this fast pace. The hated voice that called out to Big Wes confirmed my fears.

Reece Morley pulled alongside of the wagon.

"Wouldn't have any extra freight in your wagon, would you?" he called out.

"Depends on what you mean by extra. I got an extra-heavy load, and I'm late gettin' into the Springs. What you after?"

"The Deakens boy. He ran away from home this morning. I thought maybe he had picked up a ride with you. My wife is worried and so is his aunt."

"Well, now, Johnny Deakens is old enough to look out for hisself, seems to me. Been ridin' the Pass for the last four years with his dad. Might be, with John gone he just didn't want to stay around any longer."

Reece Morley's voice sharpened. "The boy's in no shape to be on his own. His sister and his aunt are pretty upset."

"Saw Aunt Marth in town this mornin'; she didn't mention anything about it."

"No, she wouldn't. We've been having trouble with him."

"Then I'd think you'd be glad to be shut of him."

Reece Morley was controlling his temper with an effort. I knew that cold, level tone of his too well.

"What I want to know is, have you seen him?"

"No."

"Any chance of his having hidden in that wagon?"

"I wouldn't know how. I opened up back at the tollgate. If he'd been there, I'd have seen him."

"You mind if I look?"

It was too late to try to get back under the tubs again. It was too late to move. What could Big Wes do if my brother-in-law showed legal papers that said I must go back with him? I cowered, not daring to breathe for the terror of the thought.

Big Wes said, "I'm behind time and it's gettin' late. Can't take a chance on this mountain road after night. You better ride on into the Springs with me. It's only a couple of miles. I've got some unloading to do there and you can look then if you've a mind to."

The bull whip cracked, the wagon jerked and started up again. Weak from the close call of discovery, I leaned back against the tubs trying to hear what Reece might say, but there was no answer.

"Where is he?" I whispered into Billy Crow's ear.

"He go 'head. No like dust."

Big Wes took up his singing again, but softer and lower.

"We're comin' to a turn,
Ridin' high; ridin' low.
There's the river right below,
Ridin' high; ridin' low.
(Hit it quick, Johnny. Follow the river up to the cave.)

Ridin' high; ridin' low.
(He's around the turn. Get out over the tailboard, fast.)
Ridin' high ridin' low."

It took me a second, but only a second, to realize that Big
Wes was singing directions to me. I didn't stop to consider how
he could have known I was there all this time, but grabbing
Billy Crow by the arm, I shoved my way out from under the
canvas in back and dropped to a squat in the dust-fogged road,
Billy Crow beside me.

The lead team was already cutting the sharp mountain curve
ahead when we snaked out of sight down over the side of the
grade and into the dense vine maple that thicketed the straight
chute into the river.

The escape was such a near thing that I lay where I was,
too shaken for a moment to move. When I started to get up,
Billy Crow put out a restraining hand.

"No move. Next time maybe he look back down-river. He
no believe Big Wes."

Thus we lay waiting until the sound of the bells and Big
Wes' singing had dimmed into the distance. Even then we slid
through the thicket like garter snakes, careful to make no stir
of branches to mark our movements. Behind a boulder at the
river's edge, we paused while I sprawled to drink, my face
buried in the cold, sweet water.

When I had slackened my thirst and had lifted my face, I
saw Billy Crow take from the pocket of his buckskin coat a
chicken bone, a scrap from our last night's supper. He dropped
it between the stones at the edge of the water. As if by some
given signal a scuttling horde of crawfish raced from their
hidden crevices, their gray shells covering the lure. Billy Crow
caught up the miniature lobsters behind their pincers, squeezed
them lifeless, and tossed them to the bank between us. When

he could catch no more, he squatted on his heels beside me, broke the tail from the body of the crawfish, and pulled out the meat. Motioning to me to do likewise, he ate it, and gave me a companionable grin.

As small children, Chelly and I had often fished for crawfish with a piece of bacon tied to a string. The way we did it was to bring the hungry crawfish slowly to the surface so that it would not let go its prize and drop back, and then to toss it quickly to the bank. Aunt Marth would then boil our catch in vinegar water and whole peppers. We thought them a great treat. But never had I eaten them raw and never had I eaten anything that tasted so good. In my shameless greed, I am afraid I ate far more than my share.

Since we did not dare go near the Springs to reach the wagon, I began to wonder how we would manage without blankets or fire. Where was this cave Big Wes had sung about? Although I had ridden over the Pass with Father for the past four years, I knew of no caves other than the ones the prospectors told about in the vast lava beds beyond the summit.

"Billy Crow," I asked, "what did Big Wes mean by 'the cave'? I never heard of a cave on this side of the mountains."

Billy Crow's stolid flat face broke into a broad grin. Black Crow, which was his true name, was a Paiute, a grandson of Chief Koonika, I was later to know. Although the Paiutes were one of the central Oregon tribes, they had used this Santiam trail through the mountains long before the coming of the white man. They had hunted and fished here before the Bannock War had driven them onto the reservation lands. If there were a cave along this trail Billy Crow must surely know of it.

In answer to my question, he pointed up the river in the direction Big Wes had driven, motioning me to follow. He started ahead, his moccasined feet sure as a wild goat's upon the boulders that lined the river's edge.

Although I was quick and agile enough, I had trouble keeping pace with him. When we came to a shallow widening of the river, Billy Crow started across, pointing out the boulders that bridged the water like steppingstones. He leaped the first two of these and waited for me to follow. My slick boots gave me no purchase and I slipped knee-deep into the water, floundering about like an awkward calf. Chagrined and angry with myself, I blundered ahead, wading the icy water the rest of the way. We came out on a sandy bank at the mouth of Cascadia Creek, a stream that ran to the back of the Soda Springs Posthouse. Big Wes would have crossed the covered bridge above here and been at the Springs by now, I was sure. And where he was, Reece Morley would be, watching until fully convinced that Big Wes had not concealed me in some manner.

How grateful I was for Billy Crow's guidance and companionship. Alone, I would have been in a sorry plight. I was grateful, too, that I felt no fear of him or enmity toward him. And more grateful to remember how Father had freed me of such fear.

"It's a man's nature to fight for his country," Father told me when explaining the terrible Indian wars just past. "Without a country of his own a man has no liberty. When the Indians saw that their hunting grounds were being taken from them, and they were being forced onto worthless reservation lands, they did the only thing they knew, they fought."

So now I followed Billy Crow confidently, treading an easy kind of deer trail, one of many such, leading to the salt licks.

Of a sudden, I heard the roar of a falls, and a turn in the trail brought us to a deep pool walled in by massive boulders. Here Billy Crow stopped for a minute. Reaching out, he broke from a nearby willow a firm but pliable branch which he tested, bending it in his hands to the half-circle of a drawn bow. Then he disappeared between a break in the boulders, leaving me no choice but to follow. Twisting and turning, I felt my way along a trail that ended abruptly at the door-wide opening of the cave.

Beyond me I could hear Billy Crow scuttling about in the darkness. Inside, the cave had the clean, dry smell of fallen leaves, but it was cold, and the thought of spending the night here in wet boots and with no fire to dry them or warm myself set my teeth to a chatter.

Billy Crow came back to the front of the cave and squatted on his heels before me. "Pretty soon make fire," he said softly. "No more cold."

Now I was to understand the meaning of the willow stick. I had never seen an Indian make fire, and it wasn't until the tiny spark finally caught in the pocket of dry leaves that I saw how it was done. Billy Crow took the buckskin thong that served as a belt from about his waist, and stretched and tied it to each end of the willow stick to make a bow. In the center of the thong where the arrow would have been nocked, he made a free loop and dropped a pointed stick of dry wood into it. He rotated this point, which rested on another piece of wood, by pulling the bow so rapidly that the friction produced a spark sufficient to light the powder-dry leaves. I saw fire made this way many times thereafter, but I was never skillful nor patient enough to succeed at it. Billy Crow blew gently on the tiny flame, feeding it with twigs until there was a secure candlelight of blaze. Now I could see the rounded dome of the cave and the heap of leaves and twigs blown in through the passage. And I could see, too, that the outcropping of rock about us was covered with carvings of running deer and horses.

We had built the fire to a considerable blaze, and I had taken off my boots to dry and was turning the inside of my pants' pockets out to the flames, when the folded map from Grandfather's journal fluttered to the floor. Until that moment I had completely forgotten it.

I picked up the page and opened it, thinking how lucky I was that it had not been ruined by the water.

In a moment of bravado, perhaps because I felt that I had not cut too brave a figure in the eyes of Billy Crow, I bent down and spread the map out with a flourish for him to see.

"This was given to my grandfather," I explained. "You see this; much gold here." I pointed to the circled spot on the drawing. "Once I get a job and can buy myself a horse, I'm going to find that hidden place," I boasted. "Even if Reece Morley takes everything away from me, I could buy back land and cattle, more than we have now. There's chunks of gold there, enough to fill a bucket. A mountain man saw it; he told Grandfather."

Billy Crow bent his black head over the map. He sucked in his breath while his brown finger traced the crooked river, marking its source. With a motion quick as a striking rattler he sprang to his feet, his words sang out a warning:

"You no go find this place. This Indian place. Great Spirit bring down big waters on white man. Walla-walla; white man die."

I shrank back from him in alarm, seeing the savage fury in his glittering black eyes. He was little older than I but strong as a grown man.

Turning his head sharply toward the entrance of the cave, as if to assure himself we were alone, he caught up the pointed fire stick like a dagger, and grasping my arm, shoved me into the blackness beyond the fire.

CHAPTER 4

THERE WAS A SOUND IN the passage to the cave. Billy Crow pushed me behind him and stood tensed, the pointed stick raised in his hand. Someone was coming toward us with soft-footed stealth. We were far enough back in the shadows to remain unseen for a second, but the fire was evidence enough of our presence. There was no place for us to run, no cover, and no escape.

Heedless of Billy Crow's warning, I made a forward grab for a burning brand and slid, flattening my back to the wall beside the entrance of the cave. If Reece Morley had found our hiding place, I knew he would come gun in hand. With the burning brand I meant to strike for his eyes. I had read in Grandfather's book of Greek legends how Odysseus had put out the eye of the Cyclops so that he and his imprisoned men might escape from the monster's cave. I was cornered and desperate and meant to fight with any means at hand.

The head that appeared around the boulder at the entrance was so startlingly unexpected that I all but dropped my stick. It was that of a dog, a small black-and-white sheep dog! When he saw the raised firebrand in my hand, he stopped short, bared his teeth and backed away, nearly tripping up the girl behind him.

"Shep," the girl cried out, pushing the dog to one side, "behave yourself."

By the light of the brand I could see that she was a strong-looking girl of about my own age, with heavy brows above wide, dark eyes. Her thick braids of hair were looped and tied to either side of her head, but, unlike my sister Chelly, she wore no bows and had no flounces and ruffles on her gingham skirts. The dog pressed his nose to her heels as she came in.

"Uncle Wes sent this," she said, giving me a long look as I tossed the firebrand back on the fire. Over one arm she carried a horse blanket, and in her hand was a tin pail with covered lid. She handed me the pail, ignoring Billy Crow who stood in the shadows beyond.

"I'm supposed to be bringing in some eggs from the milk-house in that bucket, so I'll have to wait here until you've eaten."

She dropped the blanket to the ground and sat down upon it cross-legged, drawing the dog to her, his head in her lap.

"You better hurry and eat. Your brother-in-law is prowling out around the house like a timber wolf. You'd think I was Red Ridinghood, too, the way he shows his teeth trying to make up to me."

I muttered some kind of a thank-you, without waiting for a second invitation to open the bucket. Nor did I stop until I had bolted my portion of the buttered light bread, well filled with slices of roast venison. Billy Crow, whom I motioned to the fire, squatted there, eating as heartily as myself. I was about to divide the handful of warm gingersnaps when the girl said abruptly:

"I'm Rachel Hurnden. I won't dare bring you any breakfast unless your brother-in-law leaves." Perhaps she saw the fear in my face, for she hastened to reassure me. "You're safe as long as you stay here. Nobody knows about this place except the Indians, and they don't use it any more. Not since Uncle Ed settled here and built the posthouse."

"But Big Wes knows."

"Of course. Uncle Ed found it when he was bear hunting two winters ago, and he told Uncle Wes. Uncle Ed stores his hides here sometimes when he can't get any price for them. It's dry and there's no danger of fire as there is in a barn. He doesn't want anyone to know about it on that account."

"But you know." I liked the musical sound of Rachel Hurnden's voice, and I did not want her to stop talking.

"I've lived here summers with Aunt Fannie and Uncle Ed since I was five. If they couldn't trust me they wouldn't tell me."

I breathed more freely. Still, how was I to get back on the Pass road with Reece Morley watchful and suspicious? He might go on with Big Wes or he might stay on at the hotel waiting for me. In any case I dared not leave.

"Did Reece search the freighter for me?" I asked her.

Rachel's dark eyes slitted with laughter. "He right enough did. Uncle Wes helped him. Only when Uncle Wes started to lift a stack of tubs, he let them drop on Mr. Morley's foot. Mr. Morley's boots were so soft, the tubs mashed his big toe, and he had to get out of the wagon and soak his foot in the horse trough. That gave Uncle Wes a chance to pick up the bandanna handkerchief you left under the tubs."

I reached hastily in my back pocket and surely enough my bandanna was missing. I could feel my face burning at the thought of my carelessness, and I wondered whom this forthright girl was laughing at—Reece Morley or myself. She handed me the missing 'kerchief, and I stowed it in my back pocket along with the gingersnaps, seeing that we might have no breakfast. I thanked her awkwardly and handed her the empty pail.

"If your brother-in-law starts back before the freighter pulls out, I can let you know, but Uncle Wes thinks he intends to stay." With that she started away as abruptly as she had come. At the entrance she paused. "I stay with Miss Maggie Connell in Rimrock and go to school there in the winter. Maybe I'll see you some time. I help in the Racket Store."

When she had gone I sat down again before the fire, at a loss to know what I should do next. I wondered if I dared chance getting Shone, come nighttime. If I did I would have to ride him all night, and Shone had been ridden brutally hard as it was. Then, too, Reece would know at once that I was here. No, I dared not take Shone.

In spite of what Rachel had said about the cave being unknown, I was still apprehensive and fearful of having Reece so near. I knew his slyness and his conniving persistence. My fear of being forced back to Solace and from there into prison, or what was worse, an asylum, was such that I could think of nothing but to get away. Restless and disturbed, I went a short way out of the cave between the boulders.

When I went back in, Billy Crow had curled himself up, with his back to the fire, his black head under his arm.

"Billy Crow," I urged, "wake up, quick."

He turned about and stared at me before pulling himself up on his heels. Then he motioned from the ground to his ear.

"No 'fraid. I hear if White Hair come."

"I want to get out of here before he does come. Listen, Big Wes is going to stop at Summit Meadow in the morning to put up a marker for Father. If we leave now, we can get there before he does. We'll hide. Then if Reece isn't with him, we can show ourselves, and Big Wes will let us ride on into Rimrock with him." I said "we," refusing even to consider that Big Wes might do no such thing for Billy Crow.

With a nod of willing approval, Billy Crow slid to his feet.

Pushing ahead of me, he led the way, treading pigeon-toed and silent on his moccasined feet. We did not retrace our steps but climbed the ledge down which Rachel must have made her way from the posthouse. In the clearing we skirted the log barns and outhouses, keeping well to the bordering forest until we made a half-circle to reach the covered bridge leading back across the river and to the road.

Once a dog set up a furious barking, and we were forced to flatten against the butt of a fir tree and stand still until all danger of arousing the house was over. The bright moonlight night made the apron of the bridge a hazard, lying as it did in open view of the hotel entrance, and I did not breathe freely until we were well within the depths of the covering and headed for the Pass road.

It must have been near midnight by the time we crossed the bridge and got well upon our way. Although much of the road from here on to the Summit was a climb, I was sure we could reach the place long before Big Wes, who would not start before daybreak.

The moon had dipped below the mountaintops, and the morning was graying into daylight when I finally dragged, footsore and weary beyond thinking, into the circle of meadows that marked the summit of the Cascades. We drank from the snow-water stream that laced it, before searching out a place to wait. It was Billy Crow who made our bed, in a heap of pine needles between two fallen tree trunks. Here I fell asleep, unmindful of the cold or the uncertainty of the day.

We were awakened at the same time by the sound of the freight bells and Big Wes yelling out his "Gee, haw, whoa," to the clatter of hoofs and the noise of the wagon wheels banging and sliding upon the lava rocks that marked the turnoff into the meadow.

We lay well hidden until Big Wes began to unhitch the horses for rest and water. Then cautiously I peered between the camouflage of dead branches to scan the roadway back along the rim of the mountain for any signs of Reece Morley or Shone. But the road was empty to a safe distance beyond.

Now I squirmed before the problem that faced me: What to do about Billy Crow? He had fed me, he had warmed me, and he had guided me to the safety of the cave when I needed him most. I did not want to reject him, for I had begun to feel a kinship for him as close as one might feel for a brother. But if Big Wes would not let an Indian ride with him, or refused to take me if I would not leave Billy Crow behind, what was I to do?

"Billy Crow," I whispered, "you better stay here until I call out for you. Big Wes might be cranky."

His black eyes looked at me too knowingly. "I wait."

Skirting the trees above our resting place, I came out into the meadow at the spot where the wagon was now standing. If I had expected my appearance to be a dramatic one with exclamations of surprise from Big Wes, I was very much mistaken. Other than a lift of his head and a sidewise spurt of tobacco juice, I might just have crawled down out of the wagon seat beside him.

"Well, what about some dry brush to kindle this here fire?" he boomed out at me from his place before the blackened stones of a previous camp. With that he went to the back of the freighter and took down a wooden grub box. Setting it on the ground, he lifted the lid and took out an iron pot of baked beans, a stack of sour-dough biscuits wrapped in a flour sack, and a square of comb honey.

I was back in a second with dry pine needles and an armful of broken limbs, the thoughts of hot food speeding my steps.

"That there honey, now, was a present from Rachel," Big Wes told me. "Looks like she was mighty afraid you wasn't goin' to be fed proper."

"How did she know?" I stammered, feeling myself grow red with confusion. I could see Big Wes regarding me slyly from beneath the broad brim of his old felt hat.

He shook his head at the question. "Looks like she can see farther ahead than your Aunt Marth with them ouija-board spirits she tinkers with."

Aunt Marth was a firm believer in the spiritual guidance of those who had gone before. But I was sure Rachel Hurnden must have returned to the cave before dawn and found us gone.

Big Wes laid the wood as Father and I had done in the same spot, at this very resting place. I thought of this with a dull aching pain as I looked about for the freshly made grave. No doubt it was here he had sat to clean his gun when the fatal accident occurred.

"Saw your footprints in the mud where Sweet Water Spring spilled across the road," Big Wes grunted, breaking off a sulphur match from the block in his hand. "Lucky for you Morley decided to go back home."

"You think he's going to give up trying to find me, Wes?"

"Don't think anything where that weasel-whelped varmint is concerned. He was up at daylight and went through the wagon with a fine-toothed comb. Dog kicked up a ruckus last night. Figure he thought it might have been you comin' in. Saw him from my upstairs window. He went through the barns and outhouses, the same way. But he hadn't left when I pulled out, so I don't know—" His voice trailed away in doubt. "Rachel's comin' on into Rimrock next week. Reckon she can tell us then just what he did."

He set the coffeepot on the fire to boil and squatted on his heels beside it. "What you plannin' to do when you get to Rimrock, Johnny?"

So he meant to take me on in. I didn't have to think for an answer. "I'll get a job as a herder. I always helped Father with the cattle."

Big Wes sized up my reedy figure in my cotton shirt and overalls, my hatless head of hated curls, and my shrunken boots.

"Well, son, you don't start off that easy. Not the way you did with your Pa. They'll set you trail-ending and night-herding first off, and you'll have to wrangle the cavvy."

As if I didn't know. Trail-enders were nearly always boys on their first drive who were given the tough job of riding at the end of the herd, to prod the stragglers on, choking in the clouds of dust raised by the herds ahead. When the cattle were sold at the end of the drive, the boys were left behind to bring back the cavvy of horses that had been needed for the herders, the privileged old-timers.

"I've been herding cattle over this Pass with Father ever since I could fork a saddle," I said with some heat, stung by Big Wes' doubt of me.

"Ho-o, over this Pass with two or three hundred cows and no place to turn off. That's easy. Wait 'til you start across the prairie with a thousand or more headin' into Ontario. Seen a lot of young bucks quit halfway over. Especially if they run onto a lightning storm. Work in a wagon shop looks pretty good to them after a stampede."

"Well, I'm going to get me a job riding herd to Ontario and I'm not going to quit and I'm not going to work in a wagon shop."

Big Wes stirred the bean pot thoughtfully. He lifted out a goodly portion to the tin plates, filled the coffee mugs, and ordered me to "tie in."

"What you so all-fired anxious to get on a drive for, Johnny? You'd have it a lot easier at first on a ranch near town. Maybe you think it would be safer on the move for awhile, heh?"

"No." I gulped down a mouthful of beans with a swallow of hot coffee. "I got something I want to do. There's something I'm going to find out about and nobody knows it but me."

Big Wes said, "Do tell."

I could see that he was not greatly impressed by this announcement. Stung by his indifference, I reached into my pocket and drew out the map.

"There's a place somewhere off that cattle road, a hidden place where a man can pick up gold nuggets, a whole bucketful if he's a mind to. This map shows the very spot. I'm going to get a job so I can buy a horse and grubstake myself, then I'm going into this place and get me enough gold to buy my own spread. Reece Morley can sell the cattle if he wants to. I'll buy twice as many again." I knew I was being braggardly, but I was mighty pleased with myself at the look of serious attention on Big Wes' face. He was no longer indifferent.

"Son," he said, "let's see that map."

Somewhat reluctantly, I turned the paper over to him.

He scrutinized it carefully, turning it from side to side with the good fingers of his mutilated hand.

"Wherever did you get hold of this?"

There was nothing to do now but tell him where and by what circumstances I had come upon Grandfather's journal and the map he had concealed between its pages.

Big Wes looked grave and shook his head.

"Lots of old-timers have heard about this place, Johnny."

I reached over and took my map from him and folded it hastily back. I didn't want to believe him.

"They couldn't have. I read my grandfather's journal. This mountain man that led the wagon train was the only white man who knew about it. He found it when he was trapping in there. Only the Indians drove him out. Grandfather saved his life when the pioneers wanted to lynch him. That's how he gave Grandfather the map. I guess the Indians were still dangerous and that's why Grandfather never went back. But now they are all on the reservation, or nearly all of them."

Big Wes still looked unconvinced. He pushed his hat back on his forehead and spat sideways.

"Sure, the Indians knew where it was. It wasn't money to them. It was Spirit stuff for good-luck charms. They wore them to ward off enemy arrows and the white man's bullets. But some of them did tell. Or maybe this Bold passed it on."

"Then you mean it has already been found?"

"No." Big Wes lifted the coffeepot and emptied the grounds into the fire. "Not that I've heard of."

"Then I'll find it," I declared brashly, lifted to a renewed self-confidence.

Big Wes said, "You say that map was hid in old William Deakens' journal that was stowed away in his saddlebags?"

"That's where I found it, like I said."

"And he'd writ down all about this mine and about the map."

"Yes." Hadn't I just told him that?

"And you was a readin' this book when Morley come upstairs after you? What did you do with that old book, son?"

"I just left it there on the floor under the window." I could see it in my mind's eye, lying open where I had dropped it in my escape. I didn't need to say more.

Big Wes turned about to look anxiously back up the empty stretch of road over which he had just come. He must have been thinking, as I was, that if Reece Morley had picked up that journal left open on the floor with its pages torn at the point of the disclosure of the mine and the map, he would have a double purpose in blocking my escape. For this was greater wealth than all the Deakens' lands and cattle. I knew that if he had read the journal he would never stop until he had explored every means and source to find out where I might be hiding.

CHAPTER 5

BIG WES SAID ABRUPTLY, "We've got a task to do, Johnny, and we best set about it. We've got no time to lose." I could see that he was troubled at my disclosure of the journal and the map, but that he did not want to worry me further.

"I've had no time to look about, but I don't seem to see anything to mark where John's grave might be. According to what Morley told your Aunt Marth, he put up a board slab on the spot. You take the plates down to the crick and wash up while I look about a bit."

When Big Wes had turned his back, I grabbed up a handful of biscuits and stuffed them in my pockets. It was the best I could do for Billy Crow at the moment. Then I hurried to the creek to sandscour the dirty tins for I was as eager to be on my way as Big Wes.

From the creek I could see Big Wes circling the meadow, working it over and back like a bird dog. He came up to where I was waiting at the wagon, his broad hat shoved back from his damp forehead.

"Morley's a buzzard-tongued liar; there's no board standing or lying anyplace that I can find. It's been three months but seems like there would have to be some signs somewheres."

"If Billy Crow were here," I ventured to say, "he would know where the place is."

"Then, drat his Injun skin, go fetch him out of hiding."

Without another word he climbed up on the tailboard of the wagon and began easing out a slab of marble on which I could see engraved, "John Warren Deakens, born Benton Co., Missouri, April 2, 1842. Died . . ."

The sight of the marker engulfed me in such a wave of desolation as I had never before known. There had been no services for Father and of course no burial. I realized that up to this moment I had not fully accepted his death. But here, now, was the symbol and the sureness. I turned away and stumbled toward the woods, my eyes blinded to the trail.

Billy Crow was lying still in the shadows where I had left him. I handed him the bread and told him what was wanted. It was plain that Big Wes had seen his moccasined tracks leading my own on the road.

When he had eaten his bread he got to his feet. "Now I show you."

I followed him to the wagon where Big Wes stood waiting, spade in hand. Without a word of recognition he motioned the Indian boy ahead while we followed to the far end of the meadow. Here we stopped near a clump of willows at the water's edge.

It was a strange place for Reece Morley to have chosen, in these tree roots and so close to the water. But there was the mound with the earth newly turned up and the meadow grass yet thinly green upon it.

Big Wes put down the shovel. "I'll get the marker. You come help me, Johnny."

Billy Crow shook his mane of black hair with vehemence. "No put stone here for Boss Man."

He grabbed up the fallen shovel and drove the blade into the mound. I cried out in protest at this desecration and tried to take the shovel from him, but he only drove it the deeper.

"No man here," he insisted. "White Hair make grave, put in rocks. Put ground back. No man here." He turned to face the east, reaching out his arm like an arrow to point the way ahead on the road. "You father shot up there. Way far. I show you."

My father not buried here? What did he mean by "shot"? I could only stare at him in amazement.

"You mean to tell me that John Deakens didn't shoot himself accidentally?" Big Wes yelled out, his weathered face mottled with anger. He grabbed the spade from Billy Crow's hand and for a second I thought he was going to strike the boy with it.

"Why, the humpin's hind-end of a hornet didn't you say so before this?"

I stepped quickly in front of Big Wes to face Billy Crow who stood there rigidly straight and unmoving.

"Billy," I begged, "what happened? If Father didn't shoot himself, who did? Was it Reece? Why didn't you tell us?"

"No know. No see." He continued to point ahead to where the winding road clung precariously to the mountainside, hundreds of feet above the canyon of the Santiam River. "Cows make big dust. Boss Man way front. White Hair ride behind Boss Man. Hear shot. Cows make much noise. Plenty go down into river. White Hair yell big. He say, 'stay; no let cows turn.' " He was pointing the road and pantomiming a near stampede of the cattle on the narrow road at a spot where they would have been strung out for a mile with no chance but to crowd ahead or be shoved over the edge of the road down the mountainside.

"White Hair ride back. Say Boss Man horse buck, make gun shoot, kill Boss Man."

But Shone had never bucked either my father or me so long

as we had had him. Besides, this was not the story Reece Morley had brought home to us.

"Billy, where was Father?" My heart was thumping with suspense and eagerness. "Did you see him?"

"No see. White Hair say he dead. White Hair come on here alone. He bring body."

"You never saw Father after that? You never saw his body?"

"No see."

"Then how do you know that Father isn't buried here?"

A look of slyness shadowed Billy Crow's impassive face. "White Hair say body under blanket." He pointed back to the campfire. "No blood there. No blood on saddle. When dark come White Hair come here this place. I come see.

"White Hair make hole. Put in rocks. Put ground back. No bury Boss Man."

Then the blind grave had been made beside the stream for easy access to the rocks.

"If Reece is lying, maybe Father isn't really dead," I burst out. I wanted to leave this horrible place on the run. I wanted to start in search of Father at once, back up on the road that Billy Crow had pointed out.

Big Wes shook his head, running his fingers along the welt at the back of his hairline.

"I'm afraid he is, son." He reached out his hand to press my shoulder. "Looks to me like he was shot in the back up there on that grade and that he either pitched out of the saddle down into the canyon or was rolled there. There's a gravel slide there and nothing to stop his body from sliding straight down. Morley would have had to use his own gun though." He turned to Billy Crow, looking straight at him for the first time. "Did you hear more than one shot?"

"No more shoot. Jus' one time."

Big Wes wiped a dribble of tobacco juice from the corner of his mouth with the back of his hand. "Then Morley waited and fired John's gun on his way into Solace when he was well out of earshot of you. Stands to reason." He turned back to me.

"Your Aunt Marth was sure she could smell gunpowder in the gun, Johnny. It was a thing that troubled her mightily. The powder smell couldn't have clung there from the time John was supposed to have shot it until Morley got to the ranch. She knew that. Besides, George Turner said the cattle had been held up in the meadow for three days. A lot longer than need be."

"If Reece Morley shot Father, I'll . . ." Blind fury dimmed my eyes and choked my throat. No revenge that I could think of would have satisfied my hatred at that moment.

"Whoa, there, whoa," Big Wes said softly. "I didn't say Morley killed John; I said it looked that way to me. If no one saw it happen, we got no proof of the matter. Not just yet anyway. No one's gonna take the word of an Injun, so we best find out for ourselves. Morley could swear the Injuns dug up the body. It wouldn't be the first time," he added darkly. He glanced uneasily back up the road. "We best be on our way."

I helped Big Wes with the horses and he either did not see, or pretended not to see, when I motioned Billy Crow to the wagon bed again.

When we had reached the narrow stretch in the road down which the gravel slide fanned out to the ribbon of river below, Big Wes braked the wagon to a halt. There had been three months of spring rains since my father had ridden this road, so there was little chance of any evidence to point the crime—if crime could be proved.

"Tell the Injun to look," Big Wes growled. "They got eyes like buzzards."

I did not have to repeat his demand. Billy Crow was out and poised on the rim of the mountain roadside, pointing downward.

"Plenty cow bones." He held up the fingers of his right hand. "No can see man."

Big Wes let out the length of his whip with a pistol crack that flattened the horses' ears and lengthened their necks like racers. Only the weight of the wagon held them to their pace. I grabbed the side of the wagon seat to hold on, frightened at the purple anger that swelled Big Wes' neck.

"Across the river is where Holy Joe Brennen grazes his sheep this time of year," he said finally. "Herds for Logan out of the Lost River Ranch. There's a draw on there that comes down easy to the river. When I'm freed of this load, I mean to take time off and ride into Holy's camp. John Deakens was my best friend, and if there's a trace of him there on the river, I'll set the law to knowin' why."

But Big Wes must have known, as I did, that the law was a far-distant thing, little concerned with the disappearance of one man in this wild and lonely country. Out here, men more often meted out their own laws with the Old Testament judgment of "an eye for an eye and a tooth for a tooth." Would Big Wes do that?

I wanted to ask him if I could return with him, then I remembered that I had no horse. Furthermore, I had to get a job; I could not go on forever eating from Big Wes' grub box.

We were dipping down now into the giant forests of white and yellow pine with no underbrush and only a cover of pine needles clean as a spread carpet. Big Wes took a plug of "Sawlog" from his vest pocket, bit off a sizable chew, and pouched it in his cheek to moisten. From the lower pocket he drew his watch, a big silver "turnip."

"Reckon we'll just about make Smalley's place by nightfall. We can bed down in the hay barn. Haven't had to stop there since Columbus Johnson moved out."

The road was running safely on a level with the river, and the horses needed little guiding. Big Wes leaned back, pulled his hat down over his eyes, and sang, "Down in the Valley" in his sweet womanish voice.

"Hear the wind blow, dear; hear the wind blow," he sang. "Hang your head over; hear the wind blow." And I nodded in partial sleep.

I was brought promptly awake by Big Wes yelling out, "Whoa," followed by the grind and scrape of the brakes. We had come to rest before a ramshackle hay barn braced by a lean-to cowshed, deep in manure.

Father and I had never stopped at ranch houses on our drives over the Pass, but carried our supplies on pack horses and slept in our blankets. I had seen this narrow unpainted plank house from the distant road and held no envy for its owner.

Our appearance in the unfenced barn lot acted like a clap of thunder on a bedded herd. From the open front door poured such a stream of boys and girls of all ages and sizes that I could not have counted them if I had wanted.

"Hi, you, Bub, is your Paw at home?"

Just which boy Big Wes meant would have been hard to know since they all looked alike. They might have been a flock of chickens shooed from dusting themselves in a hollow. They were all an unwashed yellow, bug-eyed, barefooted, and open-mouthed.

The spill from the doorway was plugged like a bung in a

barrel by a featherbed of a woman in a calico dress straining tight as a cinch against the bodice buttons.

"Well, howdy, Mr. Hurnden," she called out, pushing her hair up out of her eyes and pinning it to the knob on top. "Git down and come in. Mr. Smalley's abed. You young'uns now, clear out. A body'd think you never saw a freighter before."

"I ain't never," one Smalley announced, sticking out his tongue through the hole of a missing front tooth.

"You did too, Almey. You seen this very one when we stopped at Rimrock." The speaker was climbing up the back wheel of the wagon to peer under the canvas.

Just then a man came around the corner of the house stuffing his shirttail into his pants. He was a fox-faced little man with a caved-in look to his middle. He had sparse, up-standing hair the color of old straw and a big bushy moustache that hid his mouth and overshadowed what little chin there might have been.

"Well, howdy, Mr. Hurnden," he called out. "Ain't seen you since my wagon give out on me at Rimrock." He picked up a rock and threw it in the midst of the milling Smalleys. "You young'uns git out o' here or I'll take a brandin' iron to your hind ends."

"Looks like I'd have to ask you for the loan of your barn tonight, Smalley." Big Wes wound the reins about the brake handle and climbed down off the wagon.

The children scattered, some behind the house and some under the porch.

"Got delayed a bit and can't make it into Snowline before dark," Big Wes explained. "Like to bed down in the barn if it's all right with you."

"Course it is." Mrs. Smalley moved from the doorway, and the head of another Smalley emerged from the wing of her skirts. "Come right on in as soon as you've taken care of the team. I was just about to dish up."

While Big Wes was unhitching the horses, I went to the back of the wagon to tell Billy Crow of our plans. But when I lifted the canvas and called his name, there was no response. When and where he had left us, I did not know, and for the moment I confess to feeling a shameful sense of relief.

We fed the horses from our own supply of oats and watered them at a hollowed-out log propped beneath the trickle of a hillside spring. The log was green with moss, the mud about it ankle-deep from lack of drainage.

Standing at the back of the barn was a rickety spring wagon with a wheelless hub braced on a stump. There were no domestic animals in sight, although the mud about the trough was deep from their hoofs. No doubt they were back in the woods, foraging for themselves.

"Drifters," Big Wes said, eyeing the surroundings. "Stay just long enough in one spot to clean it out and then move on. Smalley's nestin' in here 'til somebody comes along to kick him out." He picked up a length of board that had been ripped from the shed and laid it across the mud up to the trough so that we could wash our hands and faces.

"Keep a weather eye on the wagon, son," he mumbled, lifting his face from the water to dry it on his red bandanna. "I don't often get caught out like this."

There seemed to be but two rooms in the downstairs of the Smalleys' house. The first was bare-floored, with a stone fireplace flanked by two rawhide-bottomed chairs. The only other piece of furniture was a roughly made table. There were no lamps, candles, curtains, or ornaments such as I had thought necessary to any house.

The kitchen was filled with a long uncovered plank table. On both sides of the table were benches where young Smalleys crowded thick as blackbirds on a rail fence. Beyond the table a cast-iron stove, its four legs elevated on blocks of wood, seeped pitch smoke from every open seam. And over all this hung a strong, unpleasantly strange odor of cooking meat.

Mrs. Smalley lifted a small boy off the bench by his suspenders, much as a cat would lift a kitten, and deposited him on the floor beside the stove. "Lola Bell," she called out, "you come here and set with Almey. Ain't you got no manners for company?"

Mr. Smalley carried an iron pot from the stove to the middle of the table. Flanking either side of it were two large milk pans. In one was mounded sour-dough biscuits speckled yellow with unmixed soda. The other pan held cold applesauce.

"Now, Mr. Hurnden, you and your boy just tie in," Mrs. Smalley invited, handing Big Wes a tin dipper and motioning to the pot. "We're having sheep meat tonight."

I thought Big Wes hesitated a moment; and as for me, hungry as I was, I could only choke with distaste—sheep meat! I had never heard of anyone but Indians eating sheep. Ham, bacon, chicken, game and trout graced our own table abundantly, with now and then a pork or veal for roasting; but sheep, never. Now that I knew the source of the smell I was reluctant to test the dish. But Big Wes helped himself to the chunks of dark meat, whole potatoes, onions, and turnips; and so did I, although lightly as I dared of the meat.

"Didn't know you raised any sheep," Big Wes remarked above the noise of pushing, snatching, and slurping.

I looked up to see Mr. Smalley's little eyes glance nervously about the room and then come to rest at a spot above and beyond Big Wes' head. He coughed and wiped his moustache with two fingers.

"Well, now, I don't. Aim to get me a few steers in here, if I decide to stay. Traded that animal off some Indians passing by. A man gets awful tired of sowbelly for a steady diet."

Big Wes looked surprised. "Injuns through here? We didn't meet any on the Pass, 'though it's about time for the salmon to start spawning in the Santiam. That usually brings 'em over. Where was these Injuns bound for? How long ago was that?"

"Oh, that was two or three months ago. Just a hunting party, I guess, no squaws."

"Paiutes, Nez Percé or Yakima, would you say?"

"Well, an Injun's an Injun, and they all look alike to me. They forded the river and went up the draw toward the Three Sisters. Had that sheep tied onto the horse, alive."

The Three Sisters were three clustered mountains that pierced the chain of the Cascades to the south within a day's ride of where we were.

"Us kids saw 'em, and we told Paw about it when he got home."

"You never did, 'cause Paw was in Rimrock when the Injuns went by."

Mr. Smalley jumped up from the table and boxed the ears of the two shoving boys, and that set up such a hullabaloo that no further conversation was possible. In the confusion I escaped from the table and the house and made my way hurriedly to the barn without waiting for Big Wes.

The lower floor of the barn was bare. When I had climbed the shaky pole ladder to inspect our sleeping quarters, I found there only a scant supply of hay, powdery dry from long storage.

"Don't trust my heft on that rickety ladder, son," Big Wes called up to me from below. "I'll bed down here near the opening where I can keep an eye on the wagon.

"Traded that sheep off an Injun," I heard him muttering to himself, "the thievin', snake-bellied, sheep-eatin' road trotter . . ."

The mow was dark in spite of a dawning full moon. With no pitchfork at hand, I scraped the hay together in a pile with my feet before lifting it to toss below. Shuffling my feet about, I found that the hay was mounded to a considerable depth in the far corner, and here it was easier to lift without raising much dust. I set about to pitch it down with the intention of making a bed of it below. With the last lift of hay, I brought up what felt like a rolled sheepskin. It was only when I had shaken it out and felt the drop of the sleeves that I knew it to be a coat. This was surely a find. I called out to Big Wes what I had discovered as I hurried to the edge of the mow to toss it down to him.

"Must be a coat Columbus left behind," Big Wes said when I had gotten back to the floor, " 'though it seems mighty soft in the hand for so old a coat."

We went out into the moonlight where Big Wes struck a match to a faggot of straw so we could look at the coat. It was then I saw the big bone buttons Aunt Marth had sewn on to replace the leather ones.

Big Wes did not have to be told that this was Father's coat. I could see that he knew it also as he stared at the blackened hole high in the shoulder.

CHAPTER 6

THE FINDING OF FATHER'S COAT left me numb with despair. Ever since leaving Summit Meadow I had clung to the hope that Big Wes could be wrong and that Father might yet be found. But here was the cruel evidence of what must have happened. Could Smalley and Reece Morley have been partners in crime? How—why?

Big Wes must have been asking himself the same question.

"Smalley could have stole it off John," he muttered, raking his two fingers through his hair, "or he could have traded it off the Injuns after they had come onto John's body and stripped it. Wherever or however Smalley got it, he got it unlawful or he wouldn't have hid it." He turned the coat in his hand to examine it more carefully.

"If the Injuns was a huntin' party like Smalley said, then they never had a sheep for tradin'. Figured to myself that Smalley's been foraging across the river at Holy Joe's camp. He'd have to ford the river close enough to that slide to see John, if John was there." With this Big Wes burst into a string of invectives.

"I'll make him tell," I cried out, feeling the hot blood of anger flood my body. "I'll . . . !"

Big Wes laid a heavy hand on my arm.

"No," he said more quietly, "no, Johnny, it would do us no good to accuse Smalley right now. Don't you see, he could swear he didn't know the coat was there. He'll deny ever seeing John just as he'll deny being near Holy Joe's sheep camp to help himself to the meat we had for supper. We can't prove he was there.

"Thought it kind o' curious that nobody asked your name at supper, or anything about you. Smalley knew me well enough in Rimrock; knew you wasn't my boy. Looks like he didn't want to bring up any questions that might concern John, now don't it?

"We'll just have to bide our time, son," he went on. "When I get shut of this freight I promise you I'll see that justice is done."

My anger slowly gave way to the old feeling of helplessness.

"But, Big Wes, how can we ever know if Reece Morley did shoot Father or not?"

"I'll know when I get back down to the foot of that slide. Keep the coat, son, but keep it out of sight until the right time comes to show it. Now you best let your mind rest on other things for tonight."

Big Wes went on convincing me to his way of action. Following his advice, I finally wrapped myself in the comfort of the warm coat and burrowed into the mound of hay for sleep. He did not follow me at once, but I heard him making some final inspection of the horses and the wagon as I dozed off.

I slept fitfully. I kept thinking of Father and how he must have talked to Reece about us. No doubt Reece knew that Aunt Marth was our only guardian during Father's absence.

From this troubled state of half drowsing, I was brought sharply awake by the sound of a horse's whinny some distance away and the answer from one of the hobbled mares at the freight wagon. I lay listening, ready to awaken Big Wes, but there was no following of hoofbeats or restlessness from the horses. The frogs, stilled by the neighing, resumed their chant to the moon. It was one of Smalley's horses, I reasoned, lured back to the barn lot by the nearness of the mares.

Now fully awake, I turned restlessly about, unable to go back to sleep. Perhaps a full half-hour had passed, I cannot say; only that I became unreasonably thirsty and could think of nothing but the watering trough on the rise behind the barn. Presently, when my thirst had become unbearable, I crept quietly from my burrow, trying not to awaken Big Wes, whose snores were muted under the broad felt hat with which he had covered his face.

My boots made no sound until they struck the plank across the mud. However, I was too far away from the front of the barn to disturb Big Wes.

Bending down over the trough, I tilted my head sideways and opened my mouth to the trickle of cold spring water.

I have no remembrance of taking one swallow, only of the shock of a powerful grip on my head that pitched me face down into the depths of the trough and of struggling and strangling in an effort to scream; of hearing in my ears the sound of the freight bells that grew louder and louder only to burst into a terrible roar. Then came the final release of black unconsciousness.

The next thing I knew I was lying face down on the grass with Big Wes bending over me.

"Wes," I rasped, "who was it?"

"Who? What do you mean by that, son? I figured you must have felt sick from the supper, seeing as you didn't take too kindly to it. I figured you must have gone to the watering trough and fainted like. Though you must have fallen in face down. What do you mean by 'who'?"

"Wes," I said, "he held my head under. When I leaned over

to get a drink he grabbed me from behind and pushed my head under and held it there."

"He? I don't see how he could have."

"Didn't you see him? Didn't you hear anything?"

"Oh, I heard someone all right. I didn't have to see him. I reckoned who it would be when I set a trap for him, a kind of alarm to warn me. Had the freight bells tied to the back of the canvas so it couldn't be lifted without enough clatter to wake the dead. Oh, I was woke up all right and when I did, I see his shirttail whippin' in the breeze around the corner of the house. Then I see your place was empty and I went searchin' for you."

"Wes, I must have heard the bells, too. I heard them just as he pushed my head under the water. If Smalley was at the wagon he couldn't have been at the trough at the same time."

"Now, that's a fact." Big Wes nodded his head gravely. "You sure it was a man's hand, Johnny?"

"It was a hard strong hand. It was no woman's hand."

"Then I reckon it's Morley, son, and there's no sense tryin' to hide from him longer. We'll take our chances with him in the open. Like as not he was scared off by the bells, but chances are he thinks he drowned you and he'll not be around here to have it look that way. You go to sleep now."

Reassured by the sight of Big Wes' whip on the straw beside his head, I sank back into exhausted sleep.

It seemed only a minute until Big Wes was shaking me awake. The horses were hitched and ready for starting.

"We'll wait our breakfast 'til we get to Snowline, son. Not that I couldn't use some hot coffee and some flapjacks right now."

Snowline was little more than a widening in the mountain road. Its one false-fronted general store was run by a man called Orie Waller. In the rear he kept a sort of roadside eating place for hungry herders, hunters and travelers going through the Pass.

By the time we reached Snowline, the sun had come out. The sharp morning air carrying the smell of fresh coffee and frying ham increased my hunger to near pain. Suddenly it dawned on me that this was no welcoming farmhouse, but a public place, and that I would be expected to pay for what I ate. Should I declare that I was not hungry or should I confess my poverty and beg for my breakfast? I jammed my hands deep in the pockets of Father's coat, embarrassed at the idea of either action.

I had searched the pockets and found them empty. But now my fingers felt a coin pressed in a corner, a four-bit silver piece. I was far too relieved to wonder how this miracle had come about. I never stopped to consider that Big Wes had warmed the coat for me before we started. So great was my relief that I resolved to get a job as soon as we reached Rimrock, that I need never be beholden to any man for my keep.

Big Wes was tying the team when the store owner came out with a coffeepot in his hand. He was a short, soft-bodied man with round blue eyes and tight curly hair parted in the middle.

"Howdy, Wes," he called out. "How come you're drivin' in here of a morning? Kinda off schedule, ain't you?"

"Had an extra load out of Solace," Big Wes explained. He gave me a gentle push forward. "This is young Johnny Deakens, Orie. Could you put us up for some breakfast?"

The storekeeper looked me over with interest. "Proud to know a son of John's. Sorry to hear about the accident. Sure, come on in; come right on in."

"How's things going, Orie?" Big Wes inquired, hanging his hat on a nail beside the door.

"No place. If I could get a price for this spread I'd sell out and go back to the valley. Injuns, peddlers, and busted homesteaders—not a thin dime between them."

Big Wes turned back to survey the empty corral before the barn. "Anyone on the road before us this morning, Orie?"

"Some Injuns headin' into Fish Lake. Too many of them runnin' loose off the reservation these days to suit me. Steal a man blind if he didn't watch out."

No more than other men on the Pass, I wanted to say. But I knew enough to hold my tongue.

"Didn't happen to hear anyone ride by in the night, did you? There's a man I'm kinda expecting to meet up with. Thought he might have passed me."

"Can't say I did, but when I sleep on my good ear I'm deaf as a post so that don't mean he couldn't have. Heard the dog fussin' a bit but she does that if a varmint comes around."

We followed the storekeeper into a small overheated room thick with the smell of a recent breakfast. A wood stove, kitchen table and open shelves filled one end of the room while at the other stood a curious round table tiered like a two-layer wedding cake. The bottom layer was a stationary rim, wide enough to hold a plate, while the second tier was made to rotate so that you did not need to ask to have the food passed but could turn the table. This pioneer invention, Big Wes informed me, was called a Lazy Susan.

The kitchen had a tidy, womanish look with scissor-fringed paper on the shelves, geranium plants in the window and a white china hen with ruby glass eyes on the Lazy Susan.

Big Wes settled his bulk into a sheep-lined chair before the revolving table and motioned me to one facing him.

But before I could be seated Orie turned about with a despairing motion of his plump white hands.

"Looks like I'm out of eggs," he said, pushing the frying pan to the front of the stove. "There's a couple of hens' nests to the back of the hayloft. I didn't gather the eggs yesterday so there ought to be some there. You mind fetching me a handful, young John, while I whittle off some of the bacon?"

Thinking to hasten the breakfast, I said I would be happy to run the errand. However, he dropped the side of bacon to follow me to the porch.

"Nest's clear to the back of the loft," he said, pointing out the barn as if I couldn't see it. "If there's none there, look under the hayrack out behind."

I hurried up the barn approach. The big double doors were closed, but the wooden peg that should have fitted the hasp to hold them together was hanging free on the leather thong at the side. I was about to lift the peg to pull open the heavy doors when I caught the strong, hated smell of fresh boot polish.

CHAPTER 7

FOR A SECOND I stood almost paralyzed, knowing that Reece was standing behind those doors waiting for me to open them. Then, more from instinct than reason, I snatched the wooden peg and dropped it into the hasp, locking the doors together behind me.

"I'll look under the hayrack first," I called back to the storekeeper, who had stopped to pick some dead blossoms from the rosebush. I was trying to make my move a natural one. I made a run for the back of the barn, praying that there was no opening there. Wherever Reece was, I told myself, Shone had to be. The barn had a solid back with only a small opening at the overhigh manure pile from which, I was sure, Reece Morley would not leave. Behind the shelter of the hayrack, I whistled softly Father's call for Shone, and the answering whinny came from the dense fir timber that pressed the clearing.

I found Shone, still saddled and bridled, and in my joy at being on him once again, I was close to forgetting my danger. But only for a second. Even if Reece should not leave the barn, Big Wes would question my absence and come in search of me.

If he came upon Reece he would need no message from me to tell him what had happened.

I headed Shone for Yellow Jacket Creek, a small stream where Father had often driven our cattle to graze. Urging

Shone into the forest, I let him pick his way around fallen trees, rotted logs and the holes in the porous lava rocks. There would be little chance of anyone but an Indian being able to track me.

Yellow Jacket Creek would guide me through a break in the mountains at the foot of the Three Sisters and back to the Santiam River. I had then only to follow the river to the shale slide where Big Wes was sure Father had lost his life. Above the slide the canyon opened to lead into the sheep camp. The isolated sheep camp would offer me a refuge if I could find no other place.

The sun began to filter through the pines. A blue jay screeched from his lookout high in a swaying treetop, and a doe leaped across the opening ahead and disappeared in a clump of rhododendrons. Pine squirrels set up a chatter of indignation at our intrusion.

Now the forest stopped abruptly before the bare black ridge of an old lava flow where nothing found root but scattered clumps of vine maple. I could smell the strong sulphur odors of the hot springs that bubbled up out of iron-reddened pot-holes to spill over and down into Yellow Jacket Creek. When we came to the top of the ridge, I saw the little stream below in a meadow that was white with Santiam lilies.

I knew I was on the right trail. Shone picked his way past the foul-smelling hot springs and down to the fresh water of the creek. I slipped from the saddle and flattened to drink at Shone's side. A small trout—a speckled beauty—all but touched my face, as I stretched over it in the water. I lay for a moment watching as others darted in and out behind the shelter of the rocks. The stream was but an arm's reach across, pebbly and clear. I imagined those trout, hot and brown on a platter before me.

Of a sudden I recalled that Father had told me how the Indians caught and cooked mountain trout. Taking off my socks and boots, I rolled up my pants. Standing ankle-deep in the icy water, I piled up stones to a height of two or more feet, making a sizable dam. Then I ran back to the timber and found a broken fir branch thick enough for my purpose. Using it as a switch, I began wading slowly forward toward my dam, switching the water gently before me as I went.

When I was within several feet of the dam, I could see the darting bodies of the trout. Dropping the thick bough down into the stream, I walked forward, holding the branches closely together, sweeping the bough before me like a net. And like a net, it caught and held two sizable trout that I was able to catch up in my bare hands. I tried a second time, and caught two more fish.

Freeing Shone of his bit, I left him to graze. Taking up the trout, I went back up the lava ridge until I came to one of the hot bubbling mineral springs. From a nearby maple bush I broke off a green forked stick, threaded my trout through the gills, and dropped them into the boiling water. When I saw them go limp upon the stick, I drew them out and ate them with pleasure. I knew I must hurry to make up for this lost time. I did not want to be caught short of the sheep camp before nightfall, with no fire and Shone an invitation to the timber wolves.

The way ahead was through a rocky high-walled canyon noisy with the spill and babble of the water. Root-washed firs and maple reached from the bank of the stream so that I had to wade, leaping boulders and leading Shone. He followed me, head down, stumbling and weary as myself, and I realized that Reece must have ridden him the better part of the night to have reached Snowline ahead of the freighter.

I came upon the headwaters of the Santiam just as the sun began to ease behind the mountains in the west. From here on I had to move with caution, bearing in mind that the Pass road followed the same course, leaving the river in view in many places. I was forced to keep in the protection of the timber wherever possible. I had no way of knowing whether Reece Morley would return this way or not.

Dusk began to smoke the light before me. The river widened, running smoother and more silently. I did not know how far I had come and now I began to fear I might not find the ford or the narrow opening leading down into the sheep camp.

At that moment a scream tore the mountains, an agonizing scream, thin and high and spine-chilling as a woman's on a rack of torturing pain.

Shone stopped so suddenly that I came near being pitched forward into the water. He stood, legs apart, trembling as from a chill. A deer came crashing out of the timber, struck the water just ahead and leaped up the steep bank on the opposite side. The cry stopped as quickly as it had come. Silence hung over the mountains still as lost time.

Oh, I had heard a cougar scream before, but always when in company with Father and always protected by fire and firearms. Now I had neither. From the way the deer had come dashing from the timber, I was sure it had just escaped and that the cougar cry was one of rage at his loss. Only a wounded or starving cougar would ever attack a man, but remembering old Stumper's scarred back and lost tail, I was afraid for Shone, or so I told myself.

I tried to think of the heroes I had read about and how they had managed to save themselves by their cleverness, but I could remember only Hercules who had slain wild animals with his bare hands. Alas, I was no Hercules. I thought of David and his slingshot. And thinking of the slingshot, I thought of Shone's bit and how it might be whirled about my head at the ends of the reins. Hurriedly, I made a hackamore of the lasso rope coiled at Shone's saddle, and slipping this over his nose, I freed the bit from his mouth. Now tying the ends of the reins together, I swung the bridle over my arm.

In this way I led Shone by the hackamore with the bit swinging, ready to strike if need be. This improvised weapon in hand gave me the courage to go on. When I reached the opening where the deer had appeared, I saw that it was a trail beaten by small hoofs. I knew they were sheep's tracks and that this must be the break leading into the sheep camp. Cougar or no, I had to chance it. The trail narrowed and soon there was only the trace of it in the failing light. Shone would have refused to follow if I had not tugged vigorously on the hackamore, pulling him forward. I dared not stop to rest, with no fire or food and a hunting cougar on the prowl. I had no idea how far to the south the sheep camp lay but reasoned it could not be far or the sheep could not have been let drift in here to water.

The climb was steeper than I had at first thought it might be, and of a sudden my legs began trembling under me as they had when I had first gotten up from the fever. Too, there was a lightness in my head that gave me a queer sensation of floating. Hanging to the hackamore, half walking and half being dragged, my ears straining into the dusky stillness, I caught the sound of a breaking twig and then a padded footfall. Shone stopped, his head lifted, his ears pointed forward. I remember screaming at him and swinging the bridle out and about my head as I stumbled forward to my knees.

When Billy Crow's words finally penetrated my consciousness, I knew that they were reassuring even though I could not piece together the full meaning of what he was saying.

"You all right now, Johnny. First I hear horse, I think mebbe it White Hair an' I hide. You yell big, then I know you, Johnny."

He was standing over me, his bang of black hair hanging between his eyes like a colt's. When I tried to struggle to my feet, he reached down to help me.

"How far?" was all I could say. "How far to the camp?"

"No far."

I let him help me to the saddle where I clung to the horn, head down, for the few hundred yards of blind riding. The canyon trail widened and leveled. I lifted my head to the glimmer of a campfire in a clearing ahead and to the barking of a dog coming across to us.

It is a strange thing that I have no memory of reaching the sheep camp or of being fed and rolled in a blanket under shelter.

When I awoke it was broad daylight. I was lying on a fir-bough bed to one side of a sizable lean-to. Between two giant pines a pole had been stretched to form the opening brace for the thatch of fir boughs that slanted back to the ground. Supplies in wooden boxes were raised from the ground on leveling stones; and across from where I lay was a bed like my own with a covering of sheepskins.

An open campfire smoked just beyond the lean-to opening and as I lay there, caring little where I was or under what circumstances, a runty-looking little man came up to the fire and sat down on a log at the edge. He was wearing a bright red stocking cap rolled tight to his head and a matching scarf wound round his neck with the ends stuffed into the top of his pants. Like Big Wes and most of the men I knew, he wore a vest but no coat. He looked near Big Wes' age. He had a long upper lip, a short blunt nose, and his half-closed eyes squinted out against the light. Reaching into his pants pocket, he took out a ball of wool and a half-finished sock and began plying his needles with expert fingers.

I lay staring at him in amazement. Not that I saw any novelty in knitting, for Aunt Marth had knitted all the socks that Father and I wore; but never had I seen a man do such work.

Perhaps the intentness of my gaze reached him, for he got to his feet and came to the opening and squinted in to me where I lay.

"Holy smokers, boy," he exclaimed, pronouncing "smokers" as if it had been spelled "schmokers," "and I thought ye'd be sleepin' the sun to bed with ye." Without waiting for me to say a word, he put his knitting in his pocket, turned back to the fire and shoved an iron pot into the coals.

Stiff and still weary, I rolled out of my blankets.

I looked anxiously about for Shone and Billy Crow, but there was no sign of either, only a scattering of sheep spreading out and up the mountainside. My throat tightened with dread that Billy Crow might have ridden away on Shone leaving me with no means of getting on my way when the time came.

"Holy smokers," Holy Joe exclaimed, seeing that I was slow to reach for the crockery bowl of rolled oats he was offering me. "Look to your belly, boy. There's plenty of time to look elsewhere."

"My horse . . ." I stammered.

"The Indian has ridden him down to the ford. An Indian has ears and eyes like a wild thing, that ye should know. He's gone to mark the spot of your father's fall. Sure now, I know the way of it, but ye can do nothing until the boy gets back, so get some strength in ye for what's to come."

I ate the cereal with brown sugar and heavy goat's cream, too sweet for my palate, and drank a cup of strong black tea, the first I had ever had; but I could not keep my eyes from straying to the path leading back from the clearing.

When I sighted Shone at the edge of the forest with Billy Crow riding bareback, his moccasined feet dangling in rhythm to the horse's trot, I pushed the empty bowl aside and raced the clearing to meet them. Billy Crow slowed and I grabbed Shone's bridle.

"You found something?" I cried out. "Was he—did you—?"

Billy Crow slid down off Shone's back and thrust the reins into my hands.

"No find."

"But, Billy," I argued, wishing I had gone instead, "if Father was shot where you say and he fell down that long shale slide, where would his body be? The river is shallow there. Even if there were animals . . ." But at such a thought I could only struggle back the sob that rose to my throat.

"No animal," Billy Crow insisted. "One horse go there. I show you." He lifted from under his loose-hanging buckskin shirt a horseshoe hooked through the thong that belted his breeches. The horseshoe was a heavy one that might have been worn by a work animal.

"Billy," I told him, "there's a drifter squatting on the old ranch just above the ford. His name is Smalley. Big Wes and I stopped to camp there night before last right after you left. We slept in his barn." Hurriedly then I told of finding Father's coat with the bullet hole in the shoulder. "Smalley's horses weren't up in a corral, so I don't know if he had a riding horse or just a team of work horses. He told us that he had traded a sheep from an Indian party. But Big Wes said if we accuse Smalley about the coat that he could swear he got it from the Indians."

"Indian pony no wear shoe. Indian no have sheep. Plenty deer, plenty fish."

"Then Smalley must have taken the coat from Father's body on his way to thieve from the camp." I now told Billy Crow of my latest escape from Reece Morley.

"He'll never stop now. He knows I doubt his story and mean to know the right of it. Was there a sign of anyone else there?"

Billy Crow pulled on his forelock of hair and did not answer.

Holy Joe stood peering at us as we came slowly back to the camp. He must have known from my dragging steps that the search had been fruitless.

"Holy smokers," he cried out, "ye got the hangdog look of a sheep killer. It's no way to face a bad situation. Now let's hear the whole of this and decide if there is nothing you can do for yourself, Johnny Deakens."

With no need for urging, I poured out my story from the day Reece Morley had ridden to our front door until my arrival at Holy Joe's.

"Ye've a great trouble on ye, and that's a fact. But, boy, ye've no need to scurry away. Ye can stay here and I'll welcome the company 'til ye decide what's best to be done."

"I know what I mean to do," I said promptly. "If Father is never to come back, if he is truly gone, then I'm going to find the mine."

"A mine!" He peered down at me in astonishment. "What mine is this ye're talking of? Ye've said nothing about a mine at all."

There was nothing now to do but tell him of Grandfather

Deakens' journal and how I had found the map of the mine between its pages. For I could see nothing to lose in telling it to a sheepherder tied here to his flock.

"An' me that's prospected for thirty years an' dug more mountain holes than a badger until the cobwebs began creeping over me eyes. And ye say ye have the map of this lost mine, Johnny Deakens?" He rubbed the palm of his hand up and over his blunt nose in what I was to know as a motion of stress and excitement. "And I've always known it was there in the fold of some lava flow—gold, cinnabar, even rubies. I've seen 'em; I know."

I had paid little attention to Billy Crow standing to one side in silence, until I heard the quick intake of his breath. He was staring at me and there was no friendliness in his black eyes. I stepped back in quick alarm. What had come over him?

"Map no good," he said. "Long time lost place. You no find."

Holy Joe could either not see the boy's dark looks, or was so absorbed in what I had just told him that he gave the words no consideration.

"Ye say ye've got the map by ye, boy?" he repeated. "Would ye care to give me a look at it, now?"

With my eyes on Billy Crow, I reached slowly into my pocket for the folded paper. It was empty.

I stood staring back at Billy Crow while Holy Joe waited, puzzled at my slowness.

Reece had my map. It could be no place else. He had taken it from my pocket at the watering trough.

CHAPTER 8

THE SILENCE WAS BROKEN by Billy Crow's long, deep sigh. It was a sigh of relief, but it flared my temper that he should feel this way about my bad luck. It had been four years since the last of the Indian wars. The Paiutes, the Bannocks and the Nez Percé had been defeated and driven back on their reservations for good. The place marked on Dan Bold's map was no longer Indian territory. What could it matter to Billy Crow whether or not I found the mine? His warning of evil spirits seemed no more sensible than the spirit guides that controlled Aunt Marth's ouija board. I threw him the bridle reins and asked him to go hobble Shone.

"Reece took the map from my pocket at the watering trough," I burst out when Billy Crow was out of hearing. "He knew I had it, that's why he followed me. He meant to do away with me so that I couldn't tell anyone else about the gold. He means to have everything.

"But I remember the way the rivers ran on the map. I remember lots of it," I insisted. "I can draw it for you. I remember exactly what Grandfather wrote about it, too."

"Can you now, Johnny Deakens, can you now?" But there was little belief in Holy Joe's voice.

Eager to prove my words, I snatched up a nearby stick and, smoothing out the ashes at the edge of the campfire, I began to draw hastily from memory what I remembered of the twists and turns of the river. Straight across the top from east to west ran the Columbia; and midway, at The Dalles, emptied the Deschutes, whose upper reaches I knew well from having forded it many times with our cattle. I remembered how the map had shown a little crooked river with a lake for its source, and a drop of falls before it emptied into the Deschutes. There were two little branches of this crooked river, and on one the mountain man, Bold, had marked the spot where the pool of nuggets could be found.

I told Holy Joe this while I traced the markings of the map.

He squatted down to squint at the tracings of my stick upon the ashes.

"That's a wicked, waterless place," he said finally. "Sure and I know it too well. Didn't I get caught in there with Old Chief Egan and a good six hundred Paiutes on the warpath right behind me. If Bold said the gold was there, it's likely to be there, for it's a gold country. If I had the eyes to see it, I'd not be here minding sheep when I ache for the feel of pick and pan in my hand."

My spirits lifted. "Mr. Brennen," I said, for I did not feel free to call him by his nickname, "if you know the country like you say and have been there, you could guide me and tell me where and what to look for. I could see for you."

He lifted his filmy eyes to mine, and he knocked on his forehead with his knobby fist as if it were a doorway to be opened to his thinking.

"Johnny Deakens," he said, excitement lending a queer lilt to his words, "Johnny Deakens, it's a deal ye've made this day."

We shook hands solemnly upon this. And we talked of our prospects and of how we were to proceed. Then, of a sudden, I remembered my empty pockets. I could not start on this trek without supplies.

It was now September. By the time I had gotten a job and earned enough money, winter would be close. In winter, the high volcanic country is a bitter snow-swept place, unfit for the exploring we would have to do.

Perhaps Holy Joe sensed my uneasiness as I fell silent.

"And what are ye thinking, Johnny Deakens, that scowls your face like a bite of quince? If it isn't enough to worry ye, I can tell ye there'll be someone else setting out to find this hidden place. Had ye thought of that? What with the map safe in his pocket, he'll waste no time, I'm thinking."

It was true. In my elation over drawing the map so accurately, I had forgotten that Reece Morley had the original, and that he would have no trouble finding someone to help him in his search. The rimrock was full of old-timers, Indian hunters, prospectors and mountain men who knew the country as well as Holy Joe. I said something of this to Holy Joe. He sat a moment in silence thinking it over, shaking his head.

"Now, from what ye tell of this pretty-mannered man with his nice clothes and taking ways, I'd say he came here from down California way. I'd say he picked up his cattle careless-like as he came, for it's easy enough if ye keep on the move. Who's to say he hasn't lost partners the same way he lost your dad? He's got to get a man that knows the country and the tracings, and he won't pick up such a one overnight." He moved over close to me as if he feared there were other ears than mine to hear.

"It's a high lava-rock country, a place not many men would dare venture into, Johnny Deakens, but I've good cause to think he'll try. There's a way to get through this Indian country —a short cut east of Logan's spread. With the Indians out of there, we'd have no cause to worry. That's how we'll get there, and get there first."

He looked at me slyly as he got to his feet. "Now, I'm think-ing Morley will go back to your homeplace to set things aright before he starts out. He'll be wanting plenty of money to see him through the search. Does it make sense to ye, boy?"

I mumbled that it did, although I was still uneasy about my lack of funds and loath to mention it.

Holy Joe did it for me. "A deal is a deal, but it's best to know where we stand. I'll have a year's wages coming to me when I drive these woollies back to Logan. It's more than ample for our needs. Now, if I find this hidden place, what's to be the share?"

"I think you should have half of it, Mr. Brennen," I said promptly. "Dan Bold told Grandfather there was gold there to be picked up by the bucketful. I want enough to buy Chelly's part of our lands so that Reece Morley can't stay there, and I want fine blooded cattle the way Father planned. I should like to buy Aunt Marth a new buggy and a pacing mare. I would like . . ." The gifts I meant to buy for Rachel Hurnden had grown to such proportions I thought it best not to mention them.

"It's generous enough, Johnny boy. I'd not ask for better terms."

The glassy-eyed shepherd dog Holy Joe called "Abel" was like no ranch dog I had ever known. He never came to camp but was fed at the distant edge of the flock he kept constantly together. Billy Crow seemed willing enough to share this labor; on what terms, if any, I did not ask. Although I knew nothing of sheep herding and like all cattlemen scorned it, I felt duty bound to share in the watch. Holy Joe was gathering the flock down out of the mountain draws and holding them in the forest-encircled clearing in preparation for the move back to the open range for winter.

It was about a week later, while I was serving a watch with Abel, that I glimpsed a rider just coming in from the river trail. Shone was hobbled below a hummock nearby. Thinking the rider to be Big Wes, I was on the point of leaping on the horse, to race bareback into camp, when Abel laid back his ears and snarled a warning. Distracted for a second, I paused. Then I saw Billy Crow sliding through the grass toward Shone. He reached for Shone's neck and the horse dropped and lay, belly down, toward the boy.

"Thief man come. You hide," Billy Crow called out softly to me.

Crouching, I made my way to where he lay, his fingers still on Shone's neck.

We were well hidden by the rise of the hummock and the intervening flock of sheep.

"Did you see him, Billy? Is it Smalley—a little man with a big bushy moustache?" We were too far away to see the man clearly.

"Thief man ride big horse, one shoe gone."

So it was Smalley. I was afraid that Holy Joe might not recognize him from my description or be able to keep my whereabouts unknown.

A sheep camp is a lonely place and a stranger is welcomed for the pleasure of his company. We saw Smalley slide from his horse and then could see no more. Shone began to lift his head restlessly, and twice Billy Crow forced him back to the ground. The sheep began drifting to the trail side of the clearing, leaving us little cover when Smalley should again mount. Billy Crow motioned the dog to round the flock back before us.

At last Smalley mounted his horse, and we saw him head back for the river path. We waited until he was well into the lip of the canyon, before letting Shone to his feet. Billy Crow slipped away into the forest, and I knew he would trail Smalley to make sure he was gone.

Feeling secure, I raced for the camp to find Holy Joe in a high good humor.

"Holy smokers, boy, I got no need to be looking for that lost mine. I got gold right here for the taking." He squinted at me, his broad mouth spread in a grin. "But where would a foxy little man with his elbows out, and riding a plug of a work horse, get a hundred dollars in gold to pay for the finding of a runaway boy? And mind ye, Johnny Deakens, the boy's a loony with a bent for killing, he says. Ye can see I'd be doing a good deed if I knew the whereabouts of such a one. Which, bad luck, I did not. It's bad news to him not to find the boy here, for he tells me it's his brother's son, left to his care, and he must leave him behind for he's driving the Pass tomorrow, taking his family to hunt greener pastures in the valley."

I could not laugh with Holy Joe. I could only stand speechless, staring at something Smalley could not have failed to see and that Holy Joe's clouded eyes had missed or did not know was there.

"Ye've no need to be taking me so serious like." Holy Joe peered anxiously at me, sensing rather than seeing my stricken face. "The fun's over and he'll not be back."

"He'll be back, Mr. Brennen, and bring Reece Morley with him." I could not keep the tremor from my voice. "Father's sheepskin coat with the bullet hole showing is hanging there on a limb where Smalley could not help but see it. He must know I am here or the coat wouldn't be here. If he is doubtful, he'll go back to the barn and find it is gone; then he'll be sure. Reece offered him the money to find me, and Smalley will tell Reece I'm here." I was close to being in a panic and could not keep my eyes from the river trail, thinking Reece might be lurking there waiting for news of the search.

"And me thinking it was a joke to laugh at."

Holy Joe came over to me and pressed his hands on my shoulders.

"Then ye must leave at once. Waste no time, Johnny boy. Ye've got two hours of sunup and by that time ye can be across the lava beds. No one but an Indian could trail ye across those. Mind what I tell ye now. Follow due east the long sharp ridge of the east Sister 'til ye come to a bubbling sulphur hole. Your nose won't let you miss it. There's a straight stairstep of holes leading down to a little lake, and there ye'll find where I made spring camp. Wait there. After this sidewinder has come and gone, then we'll start the flock moving to join ye. With a packet of grub and a blanket, ye'll fare well enough. And ye can have the lend of me rifle. Little good it does me. I've me Colt for a close shot, if needs be."

"But if Billy Crow should leave, you will have to wait for a herder." I was aware of Billy's habit of coming and going at will and, also, I knew it was the custom of the owners of bands of sheep to send in extra herders and supplies when the bands were to be moved any distance.

"I got no first sight let alone a second one," Holy Joe answered. "But I've still got Abel. Abel will be offering his eyes same as ye did. I've no need to wait for a herder. Beyond the spring camp ye can help me on in to Logan's. Now mind ye, boy, this Logan's a man with a trouble to sour him and not given to friendliness, but I'll ease the way for ye."

There was not a minute to lose. My fingers grew clumsy. In my haste I blundered and spilled, and was little help to Holy Joe who was filling my ears with advice I scarcely heard.

"Leave the coat hanging here as if it were no matter," he

insisted. "If Smalley comes back bringing your brother-in-law to ferret about, I'll say the Indian boy hung it there, and if he's here to be questioned, he can say a white man gave it to him on the Pass road."

And he gave me a scrap of blanket to pin about my shoulders to serve against the cold. When I was finally ready, I was as well-equipped as any mountain man and had little to fear once I was away from camp.

Following Holy Joe's directions I raced Shone to the clearing beyond the sheep, into the forest, and headed for the eastern slope of the Three Sisters. Once in the denseness of pines and firs, with little underbrush, I found the going easier than I had dared hope. The sheep trail was easy to follow until I came to the lava beds. Here I would lose my trail and leave no trace for Reece. I did not like to ride Shone over this wicked cutting rock, but I let him pick his way with the cunning of his Indian training.

It was dark when we finally came down into a grass plot with a trickle of spring water. Here I thought it safe to bed down until I could sight the ridge of the east Sister. I did not build a fire, but ate my biscuits cold and rolled in my blanket with Shone cropping close by for company.

A hoot owl mocked the ghostly stillness of the night and set the tiny feet of rodents scuttling to safety. And I thought of myself pursued in this same manner with no place to hide.

In the face of my helplessness I fell to weeping, both from loneliness and the aching loss of my strong, kind father. At last, wearied with grief and the happenings of the day, I fell asleep.

CHAPTER 9

THE MORNING SUN AWAKENED ME. Early as it was, the grass was dry, the air heavy with the smell of pitch and pine that promised a hot day. I crawled from my blankets and bathed my face in the trickle of cold water.

The long, sloping ridge of the middle Sister looked scarcely a mile away, but I knew that I had an hour or two of riding before I would arrive at the abandoned sheep camp.

The sun grew increasingly hot as I left the forest for the rock-strewn ridge. Here the climb was so steep that I was forced to stop often to rest Shone. When I reached the backbone of the crest running east and west, I could see down the slope to the shimmer of the small lake that was my destination. With this in sight I had no need of the sulphur holes to guide me.

The lake lay in an encircling stand of yellow pine, and beyond this stretched the plains as far as the eye could see. This was the country of wild horses, the "Horse Heaven" country. Shone was a cross-breed of this wild-horse strain and the Chihuahua spotted horse brought from Mexico by the Nez Percé. The Nez Percé knew the value of selective breeding. It was the spotted Appaloosas, their prized war horses, that had enabled Chief Joseph to escape with his people as far as the Canadian border, a trek of thirteen hundred miles. So it was a great honor for Father to have been given Shone, and I thought again that he would have sold all his fine Durham cattle before he would have sold Shone.

But I had little time to dwell on these things. There was no cooling breeze even on the high ridge, and the no-sees began stinging my face until I was forced to tie my bandanna like a veil below my eyes.

Suddenly, an inky cloud appeared, spreading until the whole horizon was a moving curtain of blackness. A far faint rumble of thunder rolled and faded into the threatening stillness. Shone laid back his ears and, when I reached my hand upon his neck to reassure him, I could feel the nervous twitching of his skin. He picked his way hurriedly forward down the ridge without my urging, while the clouds boiled up and spilled over as from some vast cauldron.

A javelin of lightning forked the sky and thunder burst like a thousand cannons at one firing. Storms such as these were common enough in the Cascades. I had no fear of them, yet I did not like being on this high exposed ridge any better than Shone. He was snorting and pulling at the bridle with such violent jerks that it was all I could do to hold him to the trail. The lightning, the thunder, the smell of nearby sulphur holes, and the strange greenish light over all, reminded me of old Reverend Osburn, our circuit-riding preacher. He had described the furies of hell to us often of a Sunday, but surely he had never experienced a storm such as this or his sermons would have made saints of all of us.

I could feel the panic in Shone's erratic lunges and I was near panic myself. By this time we had reached the leveling base of the ridge with the towering trees ahead, and beyond that was the lake, the camp and shelter. For a downpour of rain would follow such a thunderstorm as this.

Then, the lightning struck. It split the trunk of a giant pine not fifty feet ahead and lighted it as though it were a pitch stick held to a match. The flames raced the tree and exploded, throwing balls of fire into the denseness of the forest. Shone screamed the shrill horse scream of terror and, rearing straight up on his hind legs, came down with a terrible lunge, whirled, and ran with a wild and savage speed that I was helpless to control. He turned this way and that, leaping crevices, plunging through mountain streams, winding, climbing, twisting, I had no idea which way or where. I could only cling to the saddle, head down, and pray.

How long this nightmare ride lasted, I do not know. When Shone finally slowed down, I lifted my head as the willows at a river's edge raked my legs. Down this bank and through the belly-high water, Shone half-walked, half-swam to the bank on the opposite side. Here he stopped, legs spread, head down, heaving and trembling.

I did not know where I was, what river this was or in what direction we had come. From what I could see, the stream cut through a canyon above and widened here between a bench of greasewood and twisted juniper. Such willow-thicketed riverbanks were often used by the Indians as hiding places. Here, the horses could graze and water, and the tepees be pitched without being detected.

I slid to the ground and managed to loosen the cinch and lift the saddle from Shone's lathered back. When I had rubbed him down with handfuls of leaves as best I could and had left him to graze, I stripped and bathed in the tingling cold water. I washed my sweat-stained shirt and hung it in the sun to dry while I crawled back in the shade of the willows to rest.

It was plain to me now that I would have to find my way into Rimrock and from there get my directions to the Logan ranch. The forest fire would have swept across the path to

Holy Joe's abandoned camp, if not entirely over and through it. From where I lay I could not see the rise of mountains or the smoke that would mark the direction of the fire. Perhaps the rain-filled clouds had deluged the forest, as they often did following one of these electric storms, leaving no trace of fire or smoke. But the cold burn would be there for Holy Joe to discover. I prayed he might know that I had escaped and that he would not linger or turn back with the sheep, thinking to find me.

The sun was at high noon and I would have to wait for it to slant to sunset before I could be sure of my directions. I slept.

Hunger aroused me in the late afternoon and I hurried to build a fire and broil a piece of bacon from my precious packet. With this and the last of Holy Joe's sour-dough biscuit, I fared well enough. But a sharp longing for something sweet recalled the honey comb Rachel Hurnden had sent to me. I told myself that when I found the mine, Rachel would be the first person for whom I should buy a gift. Perhaps a gold locket with red and green stones like the one Reece had given Chelly and which she set such store by. Perhaps a box of candy or maybe a little lace parasol like the one Miss Fennel, our milliner in Solace, carried to church socials, although Aunt Marth said it wouldn't shade a fly. But none of these seemed gifts suitable for a girl like Rachel, and so I let my imagination have full play thinking of grand things like my mother's piano that Grandfather had had brought around the Horn for her.

This pleasant dreaming gave me such a feeling of contentment that I came near to forgetting it was midafternoon with the sun beginning to point the west, and that I must decide on my course.

Leaving the willow thicket, I climbed the rise of the ground for a better view of my surroundings. Here I could see the

Three Sisters and Bachelor Butte. The town of Rimrock I knew to be on the Deschutes and that that river ran north and south. By following the course of the stream I felt sure I would come to the river, and from there I would have no trouble finding my way.

I knew I should have to take the greatest caution, as I did not know where Reece Morley might be. If Holy Joe was right in his surmise that Reece would first go back to Solace, he would not have had time to make the return ride to Rimrock, and I was safe.

The sooner I got in and out of Rimrock the safer I would be. Since it would be useless to start on my way after sundown, I set about to fish for my supper with a hook and line Holy Joe had given me. Coming upon the lacy tracks of quail in the damp river sand, I lay in wait and near dusk killed two, which I broiled on a willow stick over the coals. Once more I slept.

The night-blooming blazing star had not closed its yellow petals to the morning light when I was up and on my way.

At the end of the day I came upon an old cattle crossing. If this was where I thought it was, then Rimrock was only a short distance away.

When, soon after, I saw the chimney smoke of the town, I hid Shone in the river thicket and sat down concealed under the bank to consider my next move.

My reflection in the water, when I leaned down to wash my face, showed my hair shaggy and sun-streaked. My face was blistered and peeled to the look of a spotted calf, half brown and half pink. My shirt was wrinkled and sweat-stained, and my woolen trousers torn and unsightly. But night would hide all that, or so I thought.

When I decided it safe enough, I crept from my hiding place beneath the bank and, leaving Shone tied for safety, made my way to the outskirts of the town. From what I could see, the few unfenced houses were closely clustered together in one or two short blocks.

Rimrock was a cattle town and had none of the gardened prettiness of Solace. It looked deceivingly large because of its double-width main street, lined with high false-fronted wooden buildings. Since it was a freight center for a good part of eastern Oregon, the street had been widened so that the freight wagons with their six-, eight- and twelve-horse teams could turn without having to unhitch.

The dozen or more street lamps lighted the crossings, leaving the center of the block in darkness. A short way down the street from where I stood, I made out the familiar sparks of a forge from an open-doored blacksmith shop, and in front of it a battered wagon with a ragged canvas covering.

The swinging doors of the saloons spilled out their brighter lights across the boardwalks to the sound of a hurdy-gurdy. Before the hitching posts stood a row of dejected cow ponies, heads down, patiently waiting.

Since the blacksmith shop was nearest, it seemed the best place to inquire about the Logan ranch, and I was in luck to find the blacksmith still at work.

Screwing up my courage, I lifted my heels and tried to walk with the purposeful air of a cowpoke, an out-of-work cowpoke, looking for a job.

The sign swinging out from the high front of the building read: "S. T. Miller & Co., Practical Blacksmiths and Horse Shoers. Hay and Grain taken in exchange for work."

When I stepped into the open-fronted doorway, the blacksmith, a strong gray-haired man in silver-rimmed glasses, was just lifting a red-hot shoe from the forge, and I watched while he plunged it hissing into the tub of water at hand.

The horse waiting to be shod was a big, clumsy animal, raw-boned and ill-cared-for. I did not see the man at its head, and when I did, it was too late. He had not worn a hat when last I saw him, but I would have known that sly, rabbity face with its tobacco-stained brush of moustache anywhere, under any circumstance. It was Smalley, the squatter.

CHAPTER 10

IT HAD BEEN ON THE POINT OF my tongue to say, "Could you tell me where the Logan ranch lies?" But the words never left my mouth. The look of amazement on Smalley's face mirrored my own. He dropped the twitch on the horse's nose, but I was out of the shop before he could take a forward step. With the terrified speed of a hound-hunted rabbit, I turned and ran blindly back up the street, the boardwalk banging to the clatter of my boots, as easy a sound to follow as a belled cat in the darkness. Close behind me I could hear Smalley's racing feet hot on the trail of my blood money.

I jumped from the boardwalk and made for the tree-hidden paths bordering the cluster of houses I had just passed. A well of blackness between two of these opened like a hole to hide me. I plunged in, stumbling and panting. At the back of the house I was forced to pause with my hand out to feel my way. A dog began barking inside, and a light came at a window destroying the security of my hideout. I ducked and darted to the rear, making for more open space, thinking to circle and strike a path that would get me back to the way I had come and the safety of the river.

A kitchen porch jutted out before me. Then, without a sound of warning, I felt myself jerked backward. A searing pain cut across my forehead, and I went down in a smothering tangle of wetness.

The dog was now barking furiously. A door banged open and a woman's voice directly above me called out in angry shrillness.

"For the land's sake, Rachel, bring that lamp out here on the porch where I can see. Sounds like a cow's got loose and run into the clothesline. Serves me right for washing so late. And bring out the broom with you. I'll get the beast out of here before it tramples the sheets in the dirt."

How much of me was hidden in the pile of wash I could not tell. I heard Smalley's voice panting and apologetic as he came running up to the beacon of the lamp from between the houses.

"Ma'am," he gasped, "I'm sorry to trouble you, but I'm looking for a runaway . . ."

He had no chance to finish. The woman's angry voice whiplashed out to the resounding whack of blows that could only have come from the flat of the broom.

"Oh, you are, are you? I know you men. Come into town and get liquored up and let your cows run loose all over the streets."

She must have been at the foot of the steps. Whack! "I'll teach you a thing or two to come prowling around a lone woman's house at night." Whack! "You get before I take a gun to you, you ornery-looking no-good trail bum." Whack!

I heard Smalley's whining, "No, now, now, you don't understand." But he wasn't staying to explain. The woman's anger followed his scuttling retreat like the sting of a hornet.

"Rachel," she continued, "light the lantern and bring out the clothesbasket. The line's down. Like as not we'll have to put all these sheets back in the boiler. I declare, I never was so mad in all my life."

"Aunt Maggie, that's the man that was in the store this afternoon with all those children. We missed a fascinator and three pairs of ribbed stockings afterward. Maybe it was the sheets he was after."

It was Rachel, Rachel Hurnden, back in Rimrock for her schooling as she had told me she would be. The angry woman could only be Miss Maggie Connell, with whom she lived.

I tried to untangle myself, lifting and struggling with the clinging mass about my head.

"Rachel!" Miss Connell had run back up the steps and now her voice was panicky. "Bring the rifle, fast; there's something alive under the wash."

Fearful of being shot at in this ignoble position, I stood up pawing desperately this way and that, calling out as best I could that I meant no harm and only wanted to be helped free. My hands finally clawed away the end of the sheets, and I pushed my head out to stare straight up into Rachel Hurnden's face, lighted by the lantern she held above her head.

At sight of me her dark eyes widened in amazement and then she burst out laughing, "Why, it's you," she said. I think she saw my humiliation, for she straightened her face abruptly and called out to Miss Connell that there was no need for a gun.

"It's a friend of Uncle Wes', Aunt Maggie, that stumbled into the clothesline."

By this time I had shed my damp cocoon and was at the steps, with Rachel halfway down to meet me. In her full bright red dress and with the lamplight shining on her black hair, I thought her handsome as a gypsy.

"And for goodness' sakes, what's a man doing in the back yard instead of at the front door?" Miss Connell came from the kitchen with an ancient rifle held at an awkward angle, ready to fire if the danger warranted. She was a peppery-looking little woman with a thin, sharp face, protruding front teeth that with her reddish coloring gave her something of the appearance of a chipmunk.

"It was Smalley," I tried to explain, "the man you just drove away. My brother-in-law sent him here to Rimrock to watch for me . . ."

"Watch for you?" Miss Connell lowered the gun and twitched around to Rachel. "What's the boy talking about? Where's he from? What has Wes to do with this? How do you know he's a friend of Wes'?" She turned about to me, leaving Rachel no time to answer. "Who you running away from and what makes you think Rachel will take you in?"

"Please, Miss Connell," I burst out, determined to be heard. "I didn't know Rachel lived in this house. I went to the blacksmith shop to ask my way to the Logan sheep ranch. This man Smalley was there having his horse shod. My brother-in-law in Solace had offered him a hundred dollars to find me . . ."

I would have gotten more attention if I had been a barking dog. I doubt she was hearing a thing I said.

"For goodness' sakes, Rachel," she interrupted, "let's gather up this wash before it's whipped to rags. I feel a wind coming up. We can thresh this all out when we get inside."

Miss Connell continued to mumble with her mouth full of clothespins, while I tried to help by gathering up the fallen wash.

"Now," she said, darting ahead to the back door, "carry this into the kitchen. At least you can do that much. What's your name?"

"Johnny Deakens."

"Never heard of you."

"I live across the mountains, over near Solace."

"Oh, that Deakens." She gave me a sharp look, and I presumed she knew of my grandfather by name, as did so many others.

"Put the basket by the stove." She motioned me ahead and I did as I was told, although awkward and abashed to be seen in such an unsightly condition before Rachel.

"Rachel," she ordered, giving me a full look, "fill the milk pitcher and bring out the spice cake. Like as not the boy hasn't had anything fit to eat for a month of Sundays. Sit over there at the table, young man, and see you don't get any crumbs on the floor. I've just scrubbed."

The newly painted floor, the brightly polished stove, the starched and ironed curtains, stiff as Chelly's petticoats, the spit and polish of everything made me so conscious of my own ragged condition that I was reluctant to sit on the ruffle-cushioned chair to which she motioned me.

"I washed in the river a while ago," I hastened to inform her.

"Eat now and talk later," she ordered, lifting the stove lids to replenish the fire. "Looks like I'd have to boil up these sheets before I go to bed."

Only good manners kept me from eating the half of the cake or drinking the whole of the milk that Rachel poured out for me.

By the time I had finished, Miss Connell had the sheets in the clothes boiler on top of the stove, and was punching them with angry stabs as if to call attention to all the trouble I had caused her.

"So this road-trotter is after you," she said above the splash and punch of her stick. "What for? You make off with something you had no business to?"

"No," I said, louder than I had intended. This time I was

determined to be heard, and rightly, for Rachel had carried my plate and glass to the dishpan and had stopped to face me, her eyes as questioning as Miss Connell's tongue.

I repeated the story of my trials from the beginning, as I had to Holy Joe. I saw in Rachel Hurnden's face a great compassion for my troubles, and so I did not spare my hardships in the telling nor the cleverness with which I had escaped the dangers of them, for I hoped for her admiration as well as her concern.

"May the Holy Saints preserve us!" Miss Connell exclaimed, giving the clothes boiler a whack that splashed the soapsuds to hissing on the red-hot stove. "How ever did you get to Joe's place?"

I told her everything except about Grandfather's journal, the map, and the true reason my brother-in-law was determined to do away with me.

"Mr. Brennen sent me on ahead to wait for him at the spring sheep camp where Smalley couldn't find me. I was going to help him with the drive. But when the storm hit the camp was burned out, and I had to come into Rimrock to find out the way to the Logan ranch. I am going to wait there for Mr. Brennen."

"If Joe Brennen had a lick of sense he wouldn't be out there alone, half-blind and only a dog for company. He ought to be in here where he could be taken care of."

I saw Rachel give Miss Connell a considered look, and I thought Miss Connell's face grew ruddier than even her poking and punching warranted.

"You can stay right here and wait," she said decidedly. "Joe can come here for you." She looked very pleased with herself at the thought.

I hastened to explain that my horse, my blanket and gun

were hidden in the willows above the town and that I would
not dare to leave them there unwatched. I pointed out that
if I were not at the Logan ranch when Holy Joe drove his
sheep back, he would surely think I had been caught in the
forest fire and would not come looking for me.

"He'll come here, you can be sure of that. And you'll get
little welcome at the Logan ranch. Logan's a soured man,
hiding himself out there and never seeing anyone. Had a
brush with the cattlemen, too, on account of the sheep. That's
why Joe grazes so far back. A cattle buyer was through here
not long ago and claimed he knew all about Logan. Said he
was a bigwig in San Francisco. He had a no-good boy that got
sent up to prison for stealing. Says Logan spent a fortune trying to get him out. Now he's hiding out there in Lost Creek
Canyon for shame, I guess."

I was little interested in this. Even though Rachel was
here, I knew I dared not tarry but must get out of Rimrock as
quickly as possible.

Rachel had had nothing to say up to now, but of a sudden
she spoke with measured thoughtfulness. "Won't this Smalley
know about your horse? If he sets folks to looking for a boy
like you on a fine Appaloosa like yours, they would spot you at
once. Even Mr. Logan might not believe you if you went out
there alone without Mr. Brennen."

"Perhaps I could hide Shone when I get near the ranch, and
walk on in."

"If you tied or hobbled him out there on the prairie, the
wolves would get him."

"I just can't leave Shone here." I was stubbornly sure on
that point.

"Then you'll have to disguise him the way the Indians do."

"Disguise him?" I had not heard of this before.

"Uncle Wes says that when the Indians can't afford an Appaloosa, they paint spots on their cayuses to make them look like an Appaloosa."

"But Shone is an Appaloosa and he already has spots."

"If you can paint them on, why can't you paint them out?"

Miss Connell did not wait for me to answer. "Well," she snapped, "why not, seems sensible to me."

And so it may have been, only I did not know how to go about it.

"Rising Sun stove polish!" Miss Connell announced, her sharp nose twitching with excitement. She reached into a little cupboard beside the stove and brought out a polishing brush and a tin of blacking.

"But," I pointed out, "Shone's spots are already black. He's a dark gray."

"Then he'll have to be black all over."

The three of us looked at the small tin and knew the answer wasn't there. It would take a gallon of such blacking to cover all of Shone's hindquarters where the spots were heaviest.

"Aunt Fannie polished the stove at the Springs with chimney soot and a bacon rind," Rachel said thoughtfully.

Miss Connell sniffed. "Fat and soot's a poor substitute for Rising Sun."

"But it would cover Shone, wouldn't it?"

Miss Connell considered this a half-second.

"A man would never think of that. Just shows you how much smarter women are than men, given a chance. Get a gallon lard bucket, Rachel, we'll shake down the stovepipe in the washroom. It needs cleaning anyway."

An hour later the blacking was mixed. Miss Connell tested it on my sun-streaked hair and pronounced it perfect.

"If Joe Brennen asks you about this, you can just tell him

Maggie Connell thought of it. I guess that will show him that it takes a woman to think a man out of trouble." Her ginger-colored pompadour shook with the vigor of this assertion.

"Rachel," she now ordered, "go bring me my long hatpin from my Sunday hat. I'd rather have a hatpin for protection than a gun any day. I'll take the lantern and walk down to the blacksmith shop. If that man Smalley is still skulking around outside, I'll run him off. If he's down at the blacksmith shop, I'll stay out of sight and come right back to let you know. I'd go for the sheriff if I didn't know he was out of town."

"If Mr. Brennen doesn't bring the sheep in at once, maybe Mr. Logan will give me a job so I can wait there," I told Rachel when the door had closed behind us. "I don't dare stay here, but I still don't know how to reach the Logan ranch."

"It's an eight-hour ride on the cattle trail south," Rachel told me, opening the pierced tin doors of a kitchen safe and taking out a platter of cold fried chicken.

"Uncle Wes freights supplies in there to Mr. Logan twice a year. The cattlemen called the place Lost Creek Canyon because the creek that goes through it just disappears under the ground and doesn't come up again. At least not where anyone has ever found. I went there once with Uncle Wes. It's awfully hard to get down to. Uncle Wes had to leave the wagon up on the rim of the canyon and take the supplies down by pack-train."

Miss Connell was back before Rachel had finished making up the shoe box of food.

"He was there," Miss Connell announced triumphantly. "He was there trying to trade Sam Miller a couple of sheepskins for shoeing his horses. Sam's not eager for that kind of trading. Now, you get going while it's safe. Tell Rachel where she can pick up the bucket." Miss Connell blew out the lamp and opened the door to the darkness of the back porch. "You could do with a hat and a pair of britches, but I don't know where I could lay my hands on anything tonight."

Rachel led the way to the front path and out to the street.

"I'm a good half-mile up the river on this side of the bend. There's a clump of cottonwood and a spread of willow," I whispered. "I'll have to leave the minute it's light enough to find the road. Smalley would know me even if he didn't know Shone."

"I've been thinking of that," she said. "I wish Uncle Wes were here. He'd know what to do."

"If Mr. Brennen should come here first," I told her, "will you tell him where I am and that I'm waiting for him?"

"Oh, he'll come sometime." I could hear the hidden laughter in her voice. "Aunt Maggie knows that; the trouble is he won't stay."

With that she thrust the shoe box in my free hand, and, without a good-by, turned and vanished in the darkness.

CHAPTER 11

IT WAS NOT SO EASY FINDING my way back in the dark, but when I had floundered about at the riverbank for some time, I whistled to Shone whose answering whinny led me aright.

This night I lay more troubled in mind than I had been since my ride out of Snowline. I knew that Reece must have sent Smalley here to look for me, thus bottling the Pass road at both ends. I felt neither safe in Rimrock nor on the trail to the ranch. One thing was certain—Smalley could never overtake me or outrun me on the miserable horse I had seen in the blacksmith shop. With that comforting thought I fell asleep.

A splash of water and the call of a bobwhite awakened me to a dim, chill dawn. I knew that a quail does not call before daybreak and that there were no bobwhites on this side of the mountains, only the California topknotted ones. I scrambled to my feet, wrapped in my blanket, and pressed back into the riverbank as far as possible. Then a rock splashed the water directly in front of me, and I heard Rachel's soft call.

"Johnny Deakens, are you there?"

I answered the bob-white call and stepped from my hiding.

Through the haze rising from the river, I glimpsed the figure coming down the bank with alarm, thinking for the moment that I had been deceived and that Smalley had found me out. I would have turned in flight if Rachel had not spoken when she did.

"I've come to help you," she said. She was wearing a man's broad black hat with a man's plaid woolen shirt over her dress.

"Here," she said, taking off the hat and shirt and handing them to me. "I borrowed them from Uncle Wes last night. He has a room over the wagon shop so I just went there and took them. When he comes back I'll tell him. The shirt is too big but you can roll up the sleeves. Aunt Maggie thinks if you cover your hair and change your shirt you'll be less apt to be noticed."

When I had brought Shone from the thicket, Rachel and I set to work brushing in the blacking. While I smeared on the greasy lumps, Rachel brushed them in, and Shone, no doubt thinking it a currying, twitched his skin in ripples of delight.

I could not help but feel regret at the loss of his spotted beauty, but it was a true disguise and I knew myself safer for it.

Big Wes' overlarge hat I padded with leaves stuffed into the sweatband until it rested, with no discomfort, above my ears. The shirt hung like a tent on my pole-thin frame, but by folding and lapping the tail into my trousers I had the look of a much heavier person.

With the job done, Rachel suggested walking ahead of me down the river to the bridge crossing. "If there is anyone at the bridge this early, I can warn you." The bridge was at the south end of Main Street and having come in on the west side of the river I had to cross there or go back miles upstream from where I had come.

Rachel gathered up the empty lard pail and the basket and I waited until she was out of sight before following. Just as I rode up out of the riverbed, she came hurrying back to warn me that there was a tent and two horses at a camping spot on the river's edge, just above the bridge.

Recalling the wagon before the blacksmith shop, I had good reason to suspect the camp was Smalley's.

"Let me up behind you," Rachel said. "With the bucket and the basket on my arm, it will seem as though we are starting to the hills for huckleberries. If it is Smalley, he'll be looking for you on a spotted horse and alone."

It seemed to me that Shone's hoofbeats had never hit bridge planking with such a thundering sound, and I found my pulse pounding to each thud until well across the bridge.

"Was he there?" I asked Rachel, afraid to turn to look.

"A man stuck his head out between the tent flaps," she said, laughing softly, "but he wasn't looking for a girl and a boy on a black horse."

When we were well beyond the sight of the town with no one following, Rachel said I was safe and she must return. She bade me farewell, and I stood on the road watching her walking straight and strong as my Aunt Marth, and I thought that I must surely find the gold mine to give her the biggest nugget of them all.

The vast desert, rimmed with a higher tableland and spread brown with bunch grass, rabbit grass and sage, stretched deceptively level to the eye. At this distance the hidden draws and gullies could not be seen. Somewhere ahead was the eroded bed of Lost Creek, and the Logan spread.

"It's a good quarter of a mile down into the ranch," Rachel had told me, "but you can't help seeing it. The trail south follows the rim of the canyon. Logan had a little trouble with the cattlemen. But down where he lives no one can get at his ranch house or feed sheds or cut off his water supply. You can't get a buckboard down into that cut, and it's too far from the rim for a bullet to carry. You go easy down that rim trail, Johnny. Uncle Wes says Mr. Logan is awfully suspicious of strangers."

All morning I had watched for eroded draws in which I might conceal myself should Smalley follow me, although up to now there had been no sign of a dust trail behind me—no horse, no rider.

Then from the corner of my eye, a flash of motion along the distant edge of the rimrock jerked me up straighter in the saddle. It was a band of wild horses, tails and manes streaming as they ran with magnificent stride. I saw them stop suddenly and swerve at the brim's black edge, nostrils flared, to gaze with disdain down into the drop below. A flash, and they were gone. Something about these animals held my eyes glued to the spot. Then I saw a rider in pursuit, two of them. They came into view bent low on their ponies, and then, as quickly, they were out of sight. Shone stopped abruptly, head up as if waiting for some sharp command.

The men on horses were riding bareback, and hatless. It had been four years since there had been any Indian trouble in this part of the country, but a thin apprehensive chill raced my spine. Father's sympathy for, and his friendship with the Indians, I well understood; but there were also Big Wes' tales of renegades and Aunt Marth's tight-mouthed recounting of ambush and murderous scalpings.

I had Holy Joe's gun, but no Indian would attack in plain sight where I would have an even chance to defend myself. I dug my heels into Shone's sides and spurred him into a run. I did not know how far I was from the Logan ranch, but prayed I was close enough so that the two could not get down off the rimrock to head me off before I could reach security.

"In Indian country," Big Wes had told me, "keep your eyes behind you same as in front. Watch the gullies and the high grass same as you would for a rattler."

Into every crevice the trail dipped, around every outcrop

of boulder I expected to see the black head of an Indian. Presently, winded, Shone slacked his gait and I, too, eased my fears. Ahead of me I saw the break in the desert floor—the yawning canyon walls that led down into Lost Creek and Logan's ranch.

When I finally came to the rim of the canyon and could look down into it, I was amazed at its depth. For from where I sat, the low, one-storied ranch house, the barn, the sheep pens and the horses corralled in their split-pole fences looked only half their actual size. It was like looking in the wrong end of a telescope.

I slipped from the saddle and, with Shone's reins in my hand, flattened on the edge of the rim. The small stream came through a gorge so deep and narrow I could only see the shadowy darkness of the basalt walls. It meandered through as lush and green a meadow as those of our own valley. A checkerboard of orchard and a row of cottonwoods flanked the sprawling one-storied ranch house.

As I lay watching, a man came from the house and made for the corral. He opened a corral gate and let out a mare and a colt to graze. At that moment Shone whinnied. The sound hit the canyon wall and echoed back to where I lay.

The man lifted his head and stood staring upward, then he turned on his heels with a slow deliberate step and went back into the house. When he came back from under the concealment of the porch I caught the reflecting flash of sunlight on metal, and I knew he had a gun across his arm. He sat down on the stoop, waiting.

The twisted trail down which I forced myself turned back and forth across the face of the rock like a bootlace, narrowed in spots to the width of a horse's body by jutting rocks too massive to be removed. Here the going was too steep for comforta-

116

ble riding and I was forced to dismount and lead Shone, with the blazing sun against the wall like a furnace. Then, making a blind turn, the cool air of the valley below swept up, bearing with it the fragrance of clover and beeswax.

When I had finally come to the foot of the grade, I found it blocked by a heavy pole gate mounted between two massive posts of rocks. Beside it stood the man with the gun. He was a tall, white-haired man with a carefully trimmed Van Dyke beard and deep-set eyes that showed little warmth or welcome.

"Well," he said, "what do you want here?"

Holy Joe had not prepared me for this.

Here in the Oregon country a traveler was a welcome guest and no questions asked. There were few locked gates and those few were to protect the cattle rather than their owners. Miss Connell had said that Logan was a suspicious man, but, even so, I had not expected to be greeted in this manner.

"I'm Johnny Deakens and I've been with Joe Brennen at the sheep camp," I hurried to say. I was suddenly conscious of the bad appearance I must be making before this man, who, though he wore boots and a cattleman's garb, had an air of being somehow above his present station.

"Mr. Brennen told me to come on ahead and wait for him here."

Mr. Logan, for it could have been no one else, unlocked the gate wide enough for Shone and myself to push through, motioning me ahead while he closed and locked the gate behind us.

"What was the reason for that?"

He stood tall above me, walking at some distance from my side, his probing gaze upon Shone, glistening unnaturally from his greasy blacking.

"My father was killed on the Santiam Pass not far from Joe Brennen's camp. I went there to hide from the man who killed Father. You see," I rushed on breathlessly, "he is my brother-in-law and . . ."

"So Joe sent you on in here. Well, it's a place you're not likely to be molested. Where's your mother?"

"She's dead, sir. There is only Aunt Marth at home with my sister. She's too old to fight Reece Morley alone, but she tried. She went to Solace to a lawyer . . ."

"Solace, Linn County? You from the valley?"

"Yes, sir."

"What was your father doing on the Pass when this Morley killed him, and what was the reason for the killing?"

I hesitated to tell him Father's business but I knew no way to avoid it.

"He was driving our cattle back to the ranch. Reece Morley was a stranger he met in Rimrock, a younger man with a small herd of beef cattle he was driving into the valley to sell. He joined Father for the drive."

"So your father was a cattleman." There was such dislike in his voice that I was forced to cry out in our defense.

"My father never harmed anybody in his life, nor took anybody's grazing lands, not even the Indians'. My father says this is a big enough country with room for all: the wild horses, the cattle and the sheep. He says only men's greed brings on fighting and warring. My father says . . ."

Mr. Logan stopped my rush of words with a short sardonic laugh and a protesting lift of his hand.

"Your father must have been proud to have such a loyal son. I'll accept your defense. You may stay until Joe brings in the sheep. We can use an extra hand or two about then."

I thought it best not to mention that Holy Joe and I had quite different aims but thanked him for the sanctuary of his house.

"There is a bunkhouse behind the kitchen where Joe stays. You will find yourself a bed there. No doubt you will be wanting your dinner."

When I had freed Shone of saddle and bridle and had turned him to the creek for water, I followed Mr. Logan inside.

The big main room, cool and dim, was flanked at one end by a mammoth stone fireplace above which hung the painted picture of a young man with dark hair and a devil-may-care look to his handsome face. On the bottom of the heavy gold frame was a disk with the name "Rodger Logan," so I thought this must be Mr. Logan's son, who Miss Connell had said was in prison.

Shelves of uneven-sized books, a great many more than filled my grandfather Deakens' secretary, crowded the space on either side of the fireplace to the height of the ceiling. An Indian blanket of scarlet and blue covered a round table on which stood an oil lamp with a brass bowl and a green shade. The floor was made of stone slabs that looked as though they had slid in place from the canyon walls above. The two big chairs near the fireplace were of red leather, deep and comfortable. Through an open door at the opposite end of the room I could glimpse the kitchen, with a fireplace instead of a stove.

"There's a basin of water on the bench beyond the kitchen door," Mr. Logan pointed out, leading me into the cool, pole-raftered room.

Then I saw that the kitchen was not empty. A man stood to one side of the fireplace looping strips of yellow dough over a stick. He was wearing a blue cotton suit with the shirttail hanging, and about his head was wound a braid of black hair. Although I had never before seen a Chinese, I knew him to be one. There was much hot talk in Solace about the number of them coming to crowd our country, though I could not possibly see how a country so vast as ours could ever be crowded. The men about the barbershop in Solace said that President Arthur would have to put a stop to their coming.

"Ah Sing," Mr. Logan said shortly, "we have a guest for dinner."

"That good." The man grinned at me. "Plenty eat. You like 'em nice duck?"

Thanking him, I hurried through the back door to the water barrel and the bench with its washbasin and roller towel. There I tried to make myself as presentable as possible. I knew I made a poor spectacle in my torn and faded clothes with my hair grown long about my ears.

When I went back in, Mr. Logan had seated himself before a bare polished table at the far end of the room and motioned me to join him. Shyness before the strangeness of the food, served from covered silver dishes such as I had never seen before, held my appetite to good manners. I ate what was served to me not knowing what it might be, and drank from a glass so delicately stemmed that I feared it might break in my fingers.

All this time I felt Mr. Logan's eyes upon me and when I had refused the last offering, he pushed back his chair, lighted a handsome pipe which Ah Sing handed him, and taking a deep draw upon it, he began to question me further concerning my affairs.

CHAPTER 12

NOW I MAY HAVE EXAGGERATED IN my telling of my abuse at the hands of my despised brother-in-law, but I spared nothing, for what is more absorbing than talking about one's self. I told him of Chelly and how her weakness for adornment had made her an easy victim for Reece Morley with his lavish gifts; and how he had later taken the jewelry away from her.

"The big diamond ring was too large for her finger, so I don't think she minded that so much," I told Mr. Logan, "but the gold cross with the red and green stones and the necklace that went with it she loved dearly and wept to lose."

"And where did this Reece Morley come from," he asked, "and how could such a young man come to possess such fine jewels, would you know?"

But I could only tell him what Reece had told Aunt Marth, which we had no way of knowing to be true. Texas was where he said he had come from, and up through California into our country looking for lands to suit his fancy.

But Aunt Marth, whose husband had been a Texan, thought this unlikely since Reece Morley did not speak like a Texan but more like a man used to city living.

"Tell me more fully, Johnny, just what this gold necklace with its cross of red and green stones looks like."

"Well, sir, it is a cross of flowers with the petals of gold and the flowers between of red stones with a green stone in the center of each. The chain is gold leaves laid flat together touching each other, and there is a stone in each leaf."

"And the ring, lad, what about the ring?"

"It is a very large stone, a diamond, Chelly says; although I never saw one so large nor Aunt Marth, either, who thinks it may be something not so fine. It was Reece Morley's mother's, and it has her name engraved inside—it says from H. S. to Alice."

Mr. Logan sat very still, staring at me until I grew embarrassed and hesitated about going on, for I wondered if he doubted what I was telling him.

Ah Sing, the Chinese cook, had paused at his work and stood with his arms crossed, his hands hidden in his loose sleeves, watching Mr. Logan with a curious intentness.

Mr. Logan said slowly, "Harry Stanford to Alice." And then, more loudly, "So he came riding to your place on your father's horse and carrying your father's gun. He came bringing the message of your father's accidental death and of having had to bury him. Yet you say the grave was empty and that the Indian boy who was a witness says the firing took place on the Pass before they came down into the meadow?"

"That is so," I insisted. "There is a slide there that goes smoothly straight down into the river. If my father was shot and fell from his saddle he would go down into the river without stopping, but Billy Crow searched and there was no sign of Father's body."

"Yet you say his coat was hidden in this man Smalley's barn loft, and you think it was taken from your father's body?"

"My father would have been wearing it. Big Wes thinks Smalley robbed Father's body and then hid the coat until it was safe to wear or sell it."

I explained again why I had not been able to follow Holy

Joe's directions as I had been told to do. How I had gone into Rimrock instead and met Smalley, who, I was sure, was sent there to watch for me.

Mr. Logan was up and out of his chair pacing the floor while I talked, and I could see that he was upset for he kept clutching and unclutching his thin white hands behind his back.

"It fits," he kept muttering. "The time is right and the man is exactly as Rodger described him: the same age, the same light hair, the same polished manners. The ring and the necklace; there couldn't be two exactly the same."

All this was very confusing to me, but if Rodger were Mr. Logan's son, the boy Miss Connell said was in prison, and Rodger had described Reece to his father as well as the jewelry Reece had given Chelly, then Mr. Logan's son must have known Reece well and have seen Chelly's jewelry. But why should Mr. Logan be so upset about this?

Suddenly he turned abruptly to face me.

"You think this man, Smalley, may follow you here?"

"Yes, sir. He knows I was with Mr. Brennen at the sheep camp. If he knows Mr. Brennen is driving the sheep back . . ."

"Yes, yes; and if he found you here, what then?"

"Mr. Logan," I cried, "if he finds me he will go to Reece Morley to get his hundred dollars and Reece will come here at once. I'm sure of that. Mr. Stover, the lawyer in Solace, gave my brother-in-law papers to make him my guardian. He told everyone that I was insane from the fever, and that I drew a knife on him. He says I should be in an asylum. If he should find me here . . . !"

"Ah, yes." Mr. Logan stroked his Van Dyke. "Ah, yes," he muttered, "then you are the bait for the trap." He scrutinized me with a curious new intentness. "But now that he has driven you from home, why is he not satisfied?"

I had promised Holy Joe that I would tell no one else about the hidden mine. "What two men know is no longer a secret," he had warned me. I stammered that I expected Reece was afraid that I would accuse him of Father's death and he would be brought to justice, which was what I hoped to do.

That he was also trying to keep me from the mine and trying to put me where I would have no claim upon it was something I dared not tell. But I was greatly worried that Mr. Logan should think of me as a bait in a trap. Did he think to hold me here until Reece could find me? Why should he want to do this?

To get away with Shone, back up the zigzag of that canyon wall, undetected, would be impossible. I was determined not to stay here as a bait to lure Reece Morley to this place. I prayed that Holy Joe might come before such time to help me out, to set us both on our way to the hidden place of our fortune.

Then it occurred to me that even if I were to ride Shone out of here, I would not dare to go back into Rimrock, and I knew nothing of the vast desert land that lay ahead to the south. Without food or water, it would be impossible to lie in wait outside for Holy Joe. And there were the Indians! What if they were renegades, some mischievous wanderers from the reservation, such as Big Wes had told me about?

Mr. Logan began his pacing again. "So far," he muttered, "he has left no trail behind him, but if this Reece Morley is who I think he is, then the devil has lured him here for his own destruction."

But if Mr. Logan meant that I was to be the lure, I wanted no part of it regardless of what it was all about.

"The name Logan may mean nothing to him and even if it did, he would feel secure since no one but Rodger knew him well enough to identify him," Mr. Logan continued to himself. "And if the jewelry . . ." He turned sharply to me. "You say he keeps this jewelry with him?"

"Mr. Logan," I assured him, "Reece carries the jewelry in his vest pocket."

"Ah, yes. And you say this horse you rode in here is your father's prize Appaloosa and that Morley took it from you? Then he would recognize it without any trouble. If he rides out here, he will, of course, look down from the rim into this place before coming in, just as you did. If he sees the horse he will be assured that you are here."

"Yes, sir, that is why I tried to hide Shone's spots with blacking."

The shadow of a smile lighted his stern face and was as quickly gone.

"So I noticed. Ah Sing, give the lad a piece of scouring soap and a brush. We will shine the horse like a jewel, for our friend Morley has a taste for jewels, and we will put him in the corral nearest the rim of the canyon where he can more easily be seen." With this he began rubbing his hands together as if delighted with the feel of them.

I could not tell Mr. Logan that Reece Morley was set upon two huntings and that I was only one of them. That would be to tell him of the hidden place, which I would never do. How could I know if Reece would set out first to find this place or if he would follow me here? Then I reasoned that the gold would do him little good if he were to hang for the murder of Father. Something told me that he would seek me out first.

"Mr. Logan," I pleaded, "I do not know why you want Reece to come here or what you mean to do, but Reece is very quick and strong, and you could not hold him if he did not want to stay. Besides, Smalley and his friend, Orie Waller, at Snowline might be with him."

"Boss," Ah Sing spoke up, "boy talk all same sense. Ah Sing no hatchet man. You no big gun fighter. Boy not big enough. Why you no wait for sheepmen to come back?"

Mr. Logan shook his white head impatiently. "A half-blind herder and a slow-moving old Mexican. What help would they be?"

But Ah Sing was determined. "Holy Joe, he ride into Rimrock, bring in sheriff man. Sheriff man find diamond ring, all these things long time lost. Then sheriff man know this man big thief. We go back San Francisco take big thief to jail. Then Rodger come home. No more trouble."

Mr. Logan came back to his chair, sat down and buried his face in his hands. After a moment he lifted his head.

"Sing," he said fiercely, "all I can think of is to lay my hands on this devil who has been the cause of our disgrace. But you are right, and so is the lad. Even if I could destroy him, I would only be destroying the evidence I need to free Rodger."

I could scarcely believe that Reece Morley was the man about whom Logan had been telling me. Yet it must be so.

Seeing the incredulous look on my face, Mr. Logan got up abruptly.

"Come with me, Johnny. I can see all this makes little sense to you."

He led me back into the big room beyond and to the fireplace directly under the portrait of Rodger Logan.

"That," he said, pointing upward, "is my son. He was not a bad boy, only high-spirited and restless, and I was too busy to give him any guidance. He met a man, older than he, who flattered him to reckless spending and debts he could not pay.

Then one night there was a jewel robbery in a mansion on Nob Hill, in San Francisco. The house was not far from our own, and one of Rodger's gloves was found beneath the window. Rodger had left the gloves at his friend's, but no one would believe his story. The description that Rodger gave me of his friend is exactly that of your brother-in-law, although he did not go by the name of Morley. And the jewelry you say he gave your sister is a part of the stolen jewelry for which my son went to prison. One piece was pawned, and Rodger's name was forged on the pawn ticket.

"If what you have told me proves true, your coming has given me such hope as I never expected to have again."

I was both sorry and glad for Mr. Logan. If the sheriff could get here before Reece I need never live in fear again. Like Mr. Logan's son, I would be free to go home. Nothing seemed more wonderful than that.

For a moment I forgot the hidden gold, and like Grandfather Deakens when tempted by Dan Bold, I wanted only the security of our valley. Then I knew that with Reece safely out of our house I would still need to replace the cattle and horses he had sold and to build back our breeding stock.

Mr. Logan began to pace the floor, his head bent forward, his hands behind his back, talking more to himself than to me.

"Joe will not be in with the sheep for several days, even though I sent Mario to help him. If this man Morley should come here in the meantime, I may not be able to hold him. In any case I need to have the protection of the law. Perhaps it would be wiser if I rode into Rimrock and brought the sheriff back with me."

"But, Mr. Logan," I protested, "what would happen if Reece came while you were gone?"

"You have a gun with you. You can use it, can't you?"

"Yes, sir, but I wouldn't want to kill a man."

"Nor do I want you to. I only want you to hold him up there on the rim and prevent him coming here until I return.

"Ah Sing," his voice was like our schoolmaster's in Solace, "pack a small bag at once. There is no time to lose."

"But time we have flour and sugar and rice. Must have coffee, too, and coal oil for lamp. Time for big wagon, I think."

"Yes, yes." Mr. Logan was impatient. "If the freighter is in town, I'll send him out."

It was one o'clock when I locked the massive gate behind Mr. Logan and saw him ride over the last turn of the trail. I had not told him of seeing the two Indians for fear of being thought a coward, but now I wished that I had, for suddenly I did not like to be here with only Ah Sing to help me guard the place. I wished with all my heart that Shone could have been left as he was, but Mr. Logan had handed me the soap and brush with orders to clean the horse at once. There was nothing to do but set about the task.

The cold water of the creek was pleasant, so, leaving my boots and socks on the bank, I rolled up my shabby trousers and led Shone into midstream for his cleaning.

When Shone was once more his proud self, I led him back to the corral under the trail rim and set upon a tour of investigation.

Curious to know where the outlet of the creek was, I followed it downstream until the sheer encircling wall of the canyon stood up before me. Streams such as these were no unusual phenomenon in this old volcanic land, that was hollowed and shelled like a blown egg, with lava crusts that cracked and opened to caves and crevices. The Indians knew them well. But here the outlet was hidden by a marsh, thick with head-high tules.

Since there was no one to forbid me, I waded into the tules, keeping close to the wall so I could hold on to the outcropping of the rock in case the water should be deeper than I thought.

The water was shallow and the rock rough enough that I could cling to it without difficulty. I waded carefully and then paused, leaning closer to the wall. I could hear the muffled sound of rushing water and knew that the outlet of Lost Creek was somewhere at my feet.

I began to feel my way more cautiously, reaching forward with my bare toes and stretching my fingers out for a firmer grip as I peered downward into the thinning reeds. I could hear the sucking sound of the water being drawn into its narrowed channel. The rock ahead jutted out to make a handhold. Flattening myself against the wall, I reached out to grasp it and swing myself forward.

With the shock of an alarm clock, a whir of rattle sounded its venomous warning so close that I let out a yell, jerked back my hand, lost my foothold, and slipped straight down into the icy water below. The tules closed over my head. I was swept into blackness and oblivion.

CHAPTER 13

I CANNOT REMEMBER THE moments that followed. I recall grasping for some solid thing on which to cling, and feeling beneath my hands and feet only the bed of smoothly rounded stones over which the water flowed.

I finally reached the dry embankment, pulled myself to safety and lay there trembling. But when I had found courage to move on a little farther from the water's edge, a wall rose to block my way. Then, as my eyes adjusted to the blackness, I could see that the passage was not blocked; that the darkness, like that at the beginning of dawn, held a dim gray promise of light somewhere beyond.

I started toward this light, my bare feet shuffling in the smooth sand, my hand against the wall. In this way I followed the tunnel for what seemed like an hour, although I expect it was half that time. The passageway now became bright enough that I could see the outline of the cavern. I began to run. Surely I had found a way out of the Lost Creek cavern!

The path made an easy curve and there it was—a wide bright circle of light pouring in from the hole of the ceiling.

Staring about, I saw that the walls were hollowed out like the inside of a ball, and curved up and over my head to the opening through which the sun was streaming. The opening was so high that there was no possible way to get out. Throwing my-self to the ground, I buried my face in my hands and wept shamelessly, helplessly. No one knew where I was. No one could reach me.

Mr. Logan might be gone two or three days. The Chinese cook would not miss me until nighttime, and he would not know what had become of me.

Getting to my feet, I began circling my enclosure. Then I noticed bits of small bones as though animals had fallen into the place and perished. Walking back to the shadowy edge of the water, I glimpsed a spot of shining blue, and when I bent over it I saw that it was a bead bored for sewing—an Indian bead. Beside the bead was a moccasin track. How old it was or how long it had been there I could not tell. Perhaps some roving Indian had fallen into this open trap.

I began walking slowly back into the dimness, following the flow of water, keeping my eyes to the sandy floor. There were more tracks here, but it became too dark to know where they led or ended.

Taking my poor courage in hand, I prayed to God in Heaven to aid me. Then, starting back into the underground darkness, I set out to follow Lost Creek wherever it might lead.

Soon the walls closed me in and the murmur of the water grew louder. I knew the stream had narrowed and deepened its channel and that I must cling close to the shelf of sand along the water's edge. It was so dark that I could only feel my way ahead. Once my foot slid into empty space and I would have pitched forward but for a handhold in the rock. I shut my eyes and held them closed, praying that when I opened them again there would be some light ahead; but there was none.

Suddenly something stirred the air gently as a fan across my face, carrying with it a strangely pungent odor, strong as an unclean barn. Soft clinging creatures filled the darkness and slid before me with thin ghostly squeaks. I had disturbed the daytime sleep of a host of bats. In a panic I screamed, flailing my arms about my head. The sound echoed and re-echoed along the hollow canyon walls. I ran stumbling forward half-crazed amid the smothering thickness of squirming, clinging bodies as I fought off the bats. My eyes shut, my hands beating the air, I stumbled. My head struck a sharp turn in the cavern wall and I fell face down upon the sand.

"Ah-eh-eh; ah-eh-eh." The cry mounted above my own and ran in through the cave. I screamed to drown it out and then, burying my face in the sand, I clapped my hands over my ears, trying to shut away what I could only think was the wailing of Indian ghosts.

"Ah-eh-eh!" It rose again. And now it ended in the sound of padding feet, of human feet coming swiftly toward me in the blackness.

I crawled to my knees and screamed wildly for help.

A candle glow of light pierced the darkness; the light became a torch held high above a head of coal-black hair that hung in a forelock between two shining eyes.

Slowly, the dimness brightened, and I knew that I would live to see the earth and sky once more.

"Little brother," said Billy Crow.

I stumbled to my feet and clung to his arm, my relief too great for words. He led the way and I followed. The miracle of his being there I had no wish to question. It did not matter. Nothing mattered but that I had been found.

The opening of the cave burst upon us from a sharp turn in the trail, leaving the stream behind.

"It is the son of Spotted Horse," Billy Crow called out ahead, and I saw squatted before a fire at the mouth of the cave an older man in tribal buckskins with beaded band across his forehead. Two pinto ponies were hobbled just outside.

The older man grunted and moved to one side, making way for Billy Crow and myself beside him.

"Little brother, you come down dark-water trail all same Indian. How you find this old hideaway place for Paiute?"

The older man had lifted his head to listen.

"I wanted to find where Lost Creek went. I got sucked inside and down the fall."

"Ah-e-e. Then you no crawl through rock like Indian?"

"How could I crawl through a rock?" I didn't know what he meant.

"Big rock hang over little rock. Under there trail for walk along black water."

Behind me the older man grunted his disapproval.

"When I got out of the water, I just followed the way it led. I was trying to get out. There were bats."

"Ah-e-e." There was laughter in his bright black eyes. "Little mouse that fly no bite man. You yell like Paiute warrior."

So it was my screaming at the bats that had brought Billy Crow to my rescue.

"How could you get here, Billy?" I wanted to change the subject. "I thought you were helping Holy Joe with the sheep."

"Mr. Logan send man from ranch to sheep camp. I follow you, then I see where fire come. I see where Shone horse ride for Rimrock, then I come for find Gray Wolf, my uncle."

It would be useless to ask him how he had known where to meet his uncle or any of his tribe, for the Indian ways of communication were no more understandable to me than the flight of birds.

Of a sudden I thought of the two Indian riders behind the wild horses. Of course, it had been Billy Crow and Gray Wolf! And he must have seen me on my way to the Logan ranch.

Was that why he was here? If Lost Creek cavern was an old Indian trail into the ranch, then perhaps Billy Crow had meant to follow me to the ranch in that way. I had a curious feeling that from the time of his coming to our house he had been watching over me, even protecting me. Father had started to bring him to us, and I wondered if he felt a debt to Father for some reason I did not know.

"Was it you I saw along the rimrock this morning?" I asked.

"Gray Wolf catch new horse for me." But he would say no more.

Gray Wolf stood up and lifted from the fire a smoke-blackened sage hen that had been roasting on a stick. He tore this apart and handed me a share of it. When I tried to thank him he only grunted his response, but I felt his approval when I ate the bird as heartily as they. The manner of eating would not have pleased Aunt Marth but it made me one of them.

The sun had slanted below the mouth of the cave when I remembered that I had been left in charge of the Logan ranch. What if Reece should come to the ranch and there was no one to stop him. He could take Shone and lie in wait for me outside.

I tried to tell Billy something of this and of Mr. Logan's troubles as I lay on the ground before the fire.

"You see, I have to go back at once but I don't know the way."

"Dark way very short," Billy Crow said, as if daring me. "This way," he pointed ahead to the west of us, "long way. Maybe come morning we ride long way."

If Billy Crow meant I could ride with him, then we would go the first thing in the morning.

Back in the shelter of the cave with a fire to my back, I slept sound as a bear in hibernation.

The sound of hoofbeats awakened me with a start. When I stared about me in the light of dawn, I saw that there was only one horse hobbled at the entrance of the cave. Gray Wolf had left us.

Billy Crow and I shared his chunk of jerky and a handful of dried fish, which we washed down with cold water from the dark and hidden Lost Creek.

The half-broken pinto did not take too kindly to his double load, and would have bucked me off if I had not clung to Billy's buckskin shirt and gripped my knees into the pony's sides. Bareback, we raced him to a fatigue that forced him to a steady gait.

By noon we came over the rise of an old land fault where we could sight the rim of the canyon that encircled Lost Creek Ranch.

I wondered if Ah Sing had gone searching for me. At that moment I was feeling something of a hero in my own eyes, thinking how I would tell this adventure to the gape-mouthed boys at school in Solace. In the telling it would be easy enough to have come through Lost Creek cavern unaided, and it would change the facts very little to ignore my terror and the manner of my rescue.

We dismounted and I took the lead down the zigzag canyon trail as I had done the day before, with Billy Crow following. When we had reached the gate at the bottom, I was surprised to find it unlocked and partly ajar, for I had locked it behind Mr. Logan the day before. Ah Sing must have opened it in search of me.

Leaving Billy Crow to hitch the pony, I raced for the back steps calling to Ah Sing that I was back.

The door to the kitchen stood open as had the gate, but there was no answering call. The house seemed suddenly too strangely still with no stir of sound beyond. I crossed the kitchen more slowly now and went into the big room. The door here was also open as was the one leading into the bedroom.

Coming into the dimness of the room from the bright sunlight, I did not see him until I was well beyond escape.

He had been standing before the window, no doubt watching my entrance into the house. His hand was on his hip, his fingers on the butt of his gun.

I tried to say something but the words would not come. I could only stand there looking the idiot he had proclaimed me.

He began to smile that hated smile.

"Well, well, Sonny; aren't you going to say hello? You're lacking in good manners, as I've pointed out before."

"What—what do you want?" I managed to croak. As if I didn't know.

"Why, now, it isn't what I want but what your sister and your aunt want. They want you to come home."

Hatred shook me to a fury of incautious words.

"So that you can have me sent to Salem. So that you can take all our lands. You lied about Father. He didn't shoot himself. You killed him. You're a . . ."

He started slowly toward me, drawing the gun, but holding the butt forward for a weapon with which to strike. He meant to beat me first. No matter what happened later, I knew he meant to give himself the satisfaction of beating me to submission.

He took off his hat and threw it behind him. I started to back away and he laughed.

At that moment the window behind him exploded. Broken glass shot across the room grazing Reece Morley's face. He whirled about to face his attacker and in a second I was through the open bedroom door with the lock turned and a chair backed under the knob. I leaned against the wall, gasping for breath. I had not expected to breathe again.

Through the window to my right I caught a glimpse of Billy Crow on the run toward the hidden recess of Lost Creek, and I knew he had thrown the rock at Reece to draw him away from me. I saw, too, what I should have noticed before: that Reece's horse was saddled and bridled at the hitching post.

There was no sound from the room beyond.

I pressed my body to the side of the wall against the danger of being fired at from the window and stood, straining my ears to the stillness of the house until I thought I could bear it no longer. Then I saw the glint of reflected light on the floor before the window and I knew that Reece was there. From the corner of my eye I saw his fingers slide along the window sash to try it. When it did not give he withdrew his hand. The weight of silence fell once more upon the house.

I thought I could hear Reece at the doorway readying for the crash. I began to feel a creeping lethargy, a weariness that would not let me stand, and I sank to the floor, my head in my hands, waiting.

At first I thought the far, faint sound was a hallucination, something dreamed from my terrible need. And then the sound grew louder, the sound of nearing freight bells echoing and re-echoing against the high rock walls.

With reckless disregard of danger, I jumped to my feet and ran to the window. Because of the porch roof, I could not see out and up the trail, but I knew by the sound of the bells that Big Wes must be at the rim repacking the team for the walk down. Then I heard the click of boot heels and I saw Reece Morley run across the porch, gun in hand, and race the path toward the gate. Here was my chance to escape. Back of me was the tule bog and the certainty now of finding the safe entrance into Lost Creek cavern on Billy Crow's heels.

Out on the porch I halted. I could picture Big Wes, un-armed but for his blacksnake whip, coming down that tortuous trail with no suspicion of what awaited him. He was Father's good friend and mine, and I would be doing a cowardly thing to run away and leave him without warning him of his danger. I had no weapon and no way of knowing what had happened to my rifle, and there was no time to search for it.

But Reece, with only a revolver, could not shoot too great a distance. He would have to wait until Big Wes was part way down the trail. If my screaming voice would carry that far, I could stop Big Wes, I was sure.

Turning back, I raced across the big room and through the kitchen. There were live coals in the fireplace but no sign of Ah Sing. Crouching before the open door, I scuttled to a hiding place behind the big water barrel on the porch.

From there I had an unbroken view of the canyon wall and the zigzag path, narrowed here and there by the outcropping of the rocks. I saw that Reece had gone through the gate and was a short way up the trail, running for the first sharp turn. I saw him stop and go back behind the projection of a boulder.

At the top of the trail Big Wes appeared in the lead of four pack horses. Before long he would have to dismount to walk the narrow turns. He hated walking and he would take his time, but sooner or later he would have to make that last turn in the trail around the rock. If I could warn him in time, if my voice would carry that far, he might hold where he was with the barricade of rock to protect him. I prayed that in that time I could find my rifle.

I knew, too, that I would have to time myself to just the right moment when the rock would be as much a protection to Big Wes as it was to Reece.

CHAPTER 14

BIG WES HAD OFTEN DECLARED THAT a man was a fool to travel afoot on two legs when the Lord had provided a horse with four. Yet before the first turn, I saw him slide off the lead horse and halt the train. When he busied himself at the pack saddle I thought he must have gotten off to tighten a cinch.

Reece had lifted and sighted his gun as if testing the distance. The flash of light from the metal was like the reflected sun on a mirror, and I prayed that Big Wes might see it.

His lead horse came on, followed by the others. Big Wes was now at the end of the string instead of leading, a strange thing for him to have done. But Big Wes was a teamster and he knew how to handle his animals. Then I realized that the horses would make the first turn around the rock that Reece was standing behind. If they balked at the sudden sight of him, Big Wes would have to come ahead to start them.

Time and again the train would halt before a narrow turn, and Big Wes would let them stand taking their time before coming on.

But every turn brought them nearer. Now Big Wes was far enough down that I could see him distinctly. I could see that he had no need to lead the pack horses, for coiled over his shoulder was his bull whip. He could use it to guide the pack as easily as he guided his freight horses.

It seemed as though I had been crouching there behind the water barrel for hours. My legs were cramped, my mouth dry.

Then, the lead horse came to the final turn in the trail where Reece stood in readiness, gun in hand, waiting.

The animal made its way cautiously, holding his pack away from the wall. It turned the corner and at sight of Reece stopped, as I had feared. Reece reached out and grabbed the hackamore and pulled it forward. The horse passed him and came on. Now the second one turned and the performance was repeated.

I knew the time had come.

The last horse started forward with Big Wes close behind. At this moment I lifted my head and screamed with all the power my lungs could bellow:

"Go back, Big Wes! Go back! Behind the rocks! He's there behind the rock. He's got a gun!"

Reece dropped to his knees and turned the gun in the direction of my voice. Then, as quickly, he was on his feet again, his arms extended, the gun on a level with his shoulder, facing the upper trail.

Big Wes slid ahead of the horse and came on. Hadn't he heard me? Didn't he know what I meant? But he must have had some idea of the danger or he would not have pressed himself so close to the inside of the wall as he was doing. I could see the butt of his whip grasped in his mutilated hand. What good would a whip do against the quick and deadly shot of a revolver?

Then I saw by the motion of his arm that he must have let out his whip, flicking it back and up the trail. The sound of the rocks that he sent tumbling out and over into the canyon could well have been caused by boot heels running in retreat.

Reece must have thought so, for he slid, arm outstretched, gun in hand, to the edge of the rock for the shot at Big Wes' retreating back.

I heard a bullet crack followed by Reece Morley's scream of pain. But the sound of the bullet was not from the gun, it was the crack of Big Wes' leaded whip.

I saw Reece bend double, grasping the limp wrist of his right hand, clawing at it, trying desperately to free it of the thong-wrapped whip. His gun was gone, flicked from his useless hand, down over the trail into the lower reach of the canyon.

Big Wes must have loosened the tension on the whip, for it dropped, freeing Reece. With that Reece turned and started on the run down toward the gate, holding his broken wrist, sidewinding blindly as he ran.

With the broken wrist and no gun he was helpless, yet so great was my fear of the man that I looked wildly about for some safer hiding place.

Before I could make up my mind which way to turn, he came heading straight toward the back porch where I crouched. He did not mount the steps but ran past me on the path to the corral. His face in passing was white as his gleaming hair, his breath coming in short broken gasps. He was making for the hitching post and his horse. With his left hand he freed the rein and managed to mount. He came back past me bent flat to the piebald gelding, spurred to a run. Now I saw his intention.

Big Wes had reached the gate on foot and was standing there, whip in hand, waiting. He could pull Reece from the saddle or he could catch and cripple the horse's legs. Reece was coming straight for him, gambling on his chances of running Big Wes down before he could be stopped.

Big Wes stood, the lifted whip in his hand. Then to my amazement I saw him make a waddling run for the safety of the gatepost and throw himself behind it. Reece swept past him, a cyclone of dust and pounding hoofs, heading straight up the trail of the canyon wall.

I couldn't believe what I had seen. Big Wes was letting him escape! I could only stand where I was, helpless, as I watched horse and rider grow smaller and smaller on the stairsteps of the trail.

It was with no kindliness of feeling but a bitterness I could ill conceal that I went forward to meet Big Wes, waddling toward me on his too-small feet. He knew that it was Reece Morley who had betrayed Father to his death and yet he had not lifted his hand to hold the man.

"You could have stopped him," I cried out when within earshot.

He didn't answer me, but went ahead to round up the pack horses heading for the creek. When he had them finally in leash, he led them to the hitching post and tied them there.

"We'll set a minute," he said, coming back to the porch and motioning me beside him.

Above us was the figure of Reece Morley halfway up the trail, still bent over like a tired old man, the horse now walking, head bent low as his own.

"You could have stopped him," I accused again. "Mr. Logan wanted him held here until he could get back with the sheriff. He's a thief as well as a murderer. Mr. Logan's son . . ."

"That I know, Johnny. I know the story, but I reckoned a dead man couldn't be made to talk, and talk he must if he's to do Logan's cause any good."

"Then why . . ."

"Why? Because I could have broken his neck the way he was comin' at me. If I felled him or if I felled the horse, he's apt to pitch over headfirst for he's got mighty little hand-holt with that broken wrist."

"But if he gets away, what good will that do Mr. Logan?" And what good will that do me, I thought bitterly. For with Reece free I could never go home, and suddenly nothing, not even the gold I might find, seemed so wonderful as home.

Big Wes leaned his back against the porch post, his eyes fixed on the figure crawling up the canyon trail. He took a plug of "Sawlog" from his vest pocket, bit off a chunk and stuffed it in his cheek.

"I'm not partial to killin' a man, Injun or white." He got to his feet with a grunt and walked to the path and stood there watching Reece, now half his size in the high blue distance.

"He can't go far with that broken wrist," he muttered. "He'll have to make for Rimrock whether he wants to or not." But I felt a tinge of uncertainty in his voice.

"I could do with a drink, son. Any water up here?"

"I'll bring you a drink."

I went down the long porch and to the water barrel at the kitchen door. I took down the tin dipper from the nail on the wall and lifted the barrel cover. I leaped back with a stifled cry, for there staring up at me was Ah Sing's corpse-blue face. Then I saw that his purple lips were hard pressed against his chattering teeth as he tried to say something. He lifted his head like a jack-in-the-box to peer behind me.

"Where he go?" he quavered.

"Reece? Up the trail. Rimrock maybe. I don't know." I gave him a hand and half-pushed, half-pulled his numb and sodden body out of the water and over the barrel top. He stood looking like Aunt Marth's old tom I had once pulled out of the well, his cotton clothes clinging like wet hair to his thin bones.

"Why you run away? Boss say not let him come in here."

"Who unlocked the gate?"

"You long time gone. I see horse far off. I think you come back so I open gate for you. Pretty soon big thief man take off his hat, then I see white hair and I think better so I get back here quick. Why you go way when boss say stay?"

Before I could answer I heard Big Wes calling out to me.

"Johnny, get here quick!"

I threw the dipper in the water barrel and ran.

Big Wes was standing at the stoop before the porch, pointing upward. "Your eyes are better than mine, son; what do you see?"

There were seven of them strung out along the rim of the canyon. They were less than child size at that distance, but I knew them for their bare heads and the way they sat their ponies—as no white man ever sat—straight-backed and heads erect, peering down upon us.

"They're Indians," I half-whispered.

"Could you tell if they've got guns?"

"I can't tell." They were wheeling away, one behind the other. "But they're coming down."

"I've heard of no Indian outbreaks nor cause for such, but the two of us down here alone and unarmed are an open invitation to trouble. No way out of here either."

"There is a way out. I don't know exactly where, but it's under the rocks down there where Lost Creek goes underground. I got swept in there yesterday and it was pretty awful. I followed the creek in the dark, then Billy Crow helped me out. He says there's a way to get into the cavern safely on the other side of the creek. The Indians know all about it. This is an old powwow place and that's the way they got in and out of here."

"Then we got about as much chance gettin' out through that as a rat in a snake hole. I tell you the truth, son, I figured Lo-

144

gan was right behind me with the sheriff all the time. Sheriff was due in from Gougheye any minute when I left. Reckoned they'd overtake me. Rachel saw Morley when he come in town last night. But Logan didn't want to make himself known 'til he had the sheriff with him to make a lawful arrest. Seemed to know Morley would head in here so he figured he couldn't miss. But I guess he did. And it looks like I've got us in a jam, son. Looks like mebby them Injuns knows Logan's gone and the place is deserted. We got to make up our minds to do somethin' and durn quick. No use holin' up in the house. Saw too many of 'em go up in smoke."

"There's the tule bog. They won't go out through the cavern because they've got their horses."

"No, that's a fact. Think we can make it without bein' seen?"

"When I looked down here I couldn't see things close to the ground at all. If we went clear along under the porch roof and then crawled—there's a spread of dry hay at the hitching post. With that over us, they'd have a hard time making us out; that is, if we didn't move too fast."

"We better move, and now."

"Wes, there's the Chinaman."

"What Chinaman?" We had started down the porch.

"Mr. Logan's cook. He's been hiding in the water barrel."

"Well, either throw him back or get him out here fast."

He went hurrying down the porch while I raced back, yelling to Ah Sing as I ran. Ah Sing was inside the kitchen bending over the fire. I grabbed at his arm to pull him away.

"Quick," I yelled, "let it go. We got to get out of here. There's a bunch of Indians up there on the rim and they're coming in."

"What matter with you? You crazy boy? Indians come here lots times, see Big Boss."

"But Mr. Logan isn't here. There's just us and we got no guns. Big Wes says come at once or stay behind."

"Where you go?"

"Out there in the high tules at the end of the creek."

"Lots snakes there. Not very good place."

"Get going. There's no other."

I had a final glimpse of the Indians on their first drop onto the trail. From that time on I was crawling on my hands and knees, leading the way first to the heap of clover hay where we covered our backs like turtles under a shell, then along the grassy edge of the creek to the bog. Big Wes was muttering and moaning under his breath as we crept in among the tules and hunched there frozen to stillness.

We could hear the resounding echoes of the ponies' hoofs on the canyon trail, sounding like a troop of cavalry horses instead of the few I had seen. But we dared not lift our hay-covered heads to peer.

"Do you think they might track us to the edge of the water?"

Big Wes grunted an angry affirmative.

The nearer the Indians came the more I doubted the security of our hiding place. Before they got close enough to see my movements I might slip across the creek to the other side where the fault in the wall opened to the cavern. I said as much to Big Wes.

"Can't take this too long," he muttered. He tried to lift his feet in the mud and I could hear the pull of his boots like the suck of a pitcher pump. "I've not got the build for this. You better get gone, son, before I start sinkin' like a sow in a slough."

Lifting my feet was now no easy task, but I was still barefooted and had not the weight of boots to pull me down.

Knee-deep in the bog, I pushed through the denseness of the tules, feeling in one place of little protection the swifter, colder flow of the water near the outlet. Here I kept safely away from the wall. Once away from the current, I began moving in toward the rocks again, slowly, fearful of the snakes that might be hidden in the warm moist crevices, but with my eyes searching these cracks and openings for the overhanging rock under which Billy Crow had said the entrance to the cavern was concealed. Perhaps it was some light and shadow, perhaps it was some movement of the tules beyond that drew my eyes to the spot. But there it was, the overhanging ledge below the level of the reeds and not too far above the water's edge. Beneath it was the water-line blackness of the entrance. I wanted to be certain that this was it before going back for Big Wes.

At that moment, thin as a startled killdee's cry, rose a keen of Indian voices. "Eh, ah, e-e-e. Eh, ah, e-e-e." The chant ended in a triumphant yell that froze me where I stood, too terrified to move.

The rush of hoofbeats thudded the end of the trail and through the gate. I could hear them hit the softness of the meadow and I knew they were coming on swiftly now. If they did not stop before the house, then they had seen our crawling movements along the creek bank into the bog.

Ahead of me lay my only hope of escape. I lunged forward to the opening.

CHAPTER 15

ON A LEVEL WITH THE WATER LINE of the bog stretched a slab of rock like a porch stoop, over which hung the rooflike projection of a larger stone. The narrow opening was under this.

Stumbling forward, I pulled myself up on this ledge.

It shames me now to know that I had no thought of anything but my own safety, such was my ingrained fear of a torturous death at the hands of the Indians. All the things my father had tried to tell me, the sympathy he felt for their plight, his understanding and friendship, were as nothing in the face of Aunt Marth's experiences and Big Wes' tales of bloody savagery.

Head bent low for the narrow opening, I dived for it. My body met the impact of another, flattening me where I was, voiceless from the impact.

"Little Brother." It was Billy Crow. He put his hands under my arms and lifted me to a half-sitting position with my back against the rock. I could see now the line of his strong white teeth in his dark face. Would he save me against his own people?

"What will they do, Billy? Why are they yelling?" I quavered.

"That Paiute song. It say warrior comes home with enemy. This old Paiute powwow place. Here Indian make big feast to dance, long time."

Who was this enemy they were singing about? Would it be Big Wes, the poor heathen Chinese and myself?

"Who do they want?" I shuddered, fearful of the answer.

"Look out, Little Brother, he is there."

He shoved me forward beyond the overhang of rock and forced me to my feet. He pushed aside a sweep of tules and I had a glimpse of the mounted Indians circled before the corral near the hitching post. There, to my horror, I saw the white, uncovered head of Reece Morley! They had captured him there on the edge of the canyon.

Reece Morley had killed my father and driven me from my home. He was the only person I had ever hated, but I did not want to see him tortured.

"Stop them. Stop them if you can," I begged.

"He belong to white man. White man will say what his Indian brothers do. You see." He was enjoying himself as if all this were a joke I could not yet understand.

But a white man with the Indians? Strain as I could, I could not see either Mr. Logan or the sheriff. Then I saw one of the men in the circle dismount—a tall, gaunt man who was so dark-skinned he might have been an Indian but for the thick black beard that covered half his face. He had on a buckskin coat, fringed pants and moccasins and his head was bare.

The circle of Indians parted for him. The chanting stopped. He walked with a painful limp up to Reece and motioned him to dismount. I saw Reece get down from his horse and lunge ahead to the porch, the bearded man behind him.

Without a warning, Billy Crow pushed out ahead of me, grasped the projection of the rock above us and leaped up and over it.

He stood there fully outlined against the canyon wall, his hand raised in motion.

"Ah-e-e," he cried out, "he is here."

With that he dropped back to the rock upon which I stood and grabbed my arm. Helpless against his strength and knowing the futility of flight, I let myself be shoved out into the tules, where he pulled me behind him like a dog on a leash.

"No 'fraid," he shouted. "The snake is broken. No poison there to strike again. You come see."

Dazed and half-aware of what I was doing, I followed.

The Indians sat their horses in a sentinel line at the hitching post facing the house. I glimpsed an old and wrinkled man in beaded buckskins, his long braids held back in the tribal manner with headband and decorating eagle feathers. Beside him was Gray Wolf.

Reece Morley was sitting on the porch, his back against the post, a thong about his waist binding him there. He was panting, his pale eyes venomous with hatred. The tall bearded man had slipped a splint of wood under Reece's outstretched hand and was binding the wrist with a piece of buckskin. He tied the two ends and turned. Billy Crow pushed me forward and stepped back.

The gaunt hollow-eyed man who faced me was a ghost: the bearded ghost of my dead father! I could only stand there staring with disbelief. It couldn't be; and yet it was.

"Johnny," he said. "Son."

"Father!" I could say no more for the strangle of unshed tears and the mounting surge of exultation.

"Father, is it really you? We found your coat with the bullet hole. We thought you had been killed."

With his hand on my shoulder he turned me about to face the line of still and silent Indians.

"Chief Koonika," he said to the old and wrinkled one, sitting proudly on his spotted horse, "this is my son who wishes to thank you for my safe return. He is young and his words are small but his heart is full.

"Johnny," he said softly, "thank this man as you would a man of greatness and a friend. I owe my life to him."

What words I used I cannot recall. But I think I knew, then, that never again would I fear any man for his blood or his customs.

It has been twenty years since I saw that walled-in canyon where my father found me, but I can see it at this moment as clearly as if it were today: Old Chief Koonika sitting his horse, royal as any king upon his throne. And Father's hand upon Billy Crow's shoulder as well as my own, telling of his pride and trust in the Indian boy. It was then I learned that Father had been bringing Billy Crow home with him to teach him animal husbandry. It was Billy Crow who had come upon the tracks on the banks of the Santiam and knew they were made by Indian ponies. But he did not know whether Indians had carried Father away to bury him or save him and he was reluctant to tell me of his find. When I was forced to leave the sheep camp, Billy Crow had followed the trail of the hunters, and had come upon Gray Wolf and learned that Father was alive, having lain for months with a broken leg, his memory gone. The shoulder wound had been a minor one.

Billy Crow knew I would be making for the Logan ranch and had been watching for me on the rimrock. He had ridden to the cave meaning to join me at the ranch. Only I had reached him first through my misadventure. It was from there Gray Wolf had set out to bring Father to my aid.

Our questions and answers were stopped by the far sound of newer arrivals on the canyon trail. Two horsemen were coming down.

Chief Koonika and his men sat impassive and unconcerned, well aware of the approaching men.

I thought I recognized Mr. Logan from his palomino mount and knew the rider behind him must be the sheriff.

"It's Mr. Logan," I told Father, "Mr. Logan and the sheriff."

"Hurry to the gate, Johnny," Father told me. "Meet the sheriff and tell him that these are friends who came to our aid."

"Father is here," I shouted to Mr. Logan who came up to me first at the gate. "The Indians found him and kept him alive. Reece came, but Big Wes whipped his gun out of his hand and broke his wrist. He's here."

"Thought for a time the Paiutes had decided to take over here again," said the sheriff. "Let's go along, Logan, and finish this thing up."

Until that moment, I had given no thought to Big Wes or Ah Sing, but when I got back to where Mr. Logan and the sheriff dismounted, I saw that Big Wes, mud-covered and disheveled, had joined them, and that Ah Sing was shuffling down the porch toward the kitchen leaving a rat-tailed mark of water behind him.

But something was amiss.

Billy Crow was speaking to the chief in rapid guttural phrases that set a scowl upon the old man's face.

I saw Father's face darken as he turned about to stare first at Reece Morley and then at myself, and I knew he understood the words that were being spoken.

"Johnny," he said, "what is the evil thing that Morley has taken from you?"

In my joy at having Father back and my relief at having my troubles end, I might never have thought of the map of the hidden place until I was safely back home. But now I could hear the muttering of the men beside old Chief Koonika and I knew they were waiting for my answer.

"It is the map Reece stole from me at the Smalley ranch the night he tried to drown me."

"What map are you talking about, Johnny? What does Morley want with it?"

"It is Grandfather's map. I found it between the pages of his journal. It's the one the mountain man, Dan Bold, gave Grandfather. Bold told Grandfather the map showed a place where gold nuggets were so thick they could be scooped up with a bucket. He said—"

"Morley, have you got that map on you?"

Reece did not lift his sullen face nor did he answer.

"Johnny," Father commanded, "search him."

I had little wish to lay my hands on Reece Morley, now that I was safe, but I did as I was told. I drew the map from his vest pocket, folded just as he had taken it from me, feeling him ease back in relief as I did so.

Father took the paper from me, glanced at it, and then with a quiet word to old Koonika he tore the map into many pieces and set them scattering on the breeze into the current of Lost Creek.

It was true that I had drawn the map from memory and could do it again, but I knew Father would have none of the Indian gold. The secret was to be kept, the hidden place unfound, and I thought with a spasm of regret that I would have been satisfied if only I could have seen just one chunk of gold from the treasure trove; one fine piece for Rachel.

Mr. Logan's authoritative voice cut the thread of my thoughts.

"And now, Mr. Deakens, with your permission, I have a matter of my own to settle. Johnny, would you be kind enough to empty all of Morley's pockets of their possessions? I recall you spoke of his keeping your sister's gifts of jewelry with him at all times. I am curious to see that jewelry, Mr. Morley."

Morley made an involuntary motion with his broken hand to his empty holster.

There was a tense alertness in those around me as I emptied Reece Morley's pockets, vest and trousers, but there was no chamois bag.

I could feel Morley's twitching muscles ease. Mr. Logan looked suddenly old, tired and spiritless.

When Chelly and I were very small and she had taken more than her share of horehound drops or licorice bits, I could always ferret out their hiding place by starting forward quickly at her as if I meant to take them from her. Then she would clutch the apron pocket in which the candy was concealed. I remembered this when Reece Morley moved his hand to his holster.

I turned sharply on my heel and reached for the empty holster at his gun belt.

His left hand struck out at me, hitting me across the face with a blow that staggered me backward, blinding me for a moment.

"They're in his holster," I cried out to Mr. Logan.

When I could bring my blinking eyes to focus, I saw Chelly's pretties, a glittering heap in Mr. Logan's hands.

Then Mr. Logan spoke out, commanding our attention.

"You are all witness to the finding of these stolen jewels." He turned directly to Father. "There is considerable reward for their return. On top of that, I myself have offered ten thousand dollars for the apprehension of this man, Morley, alive. Your son has earned the first reward and you the second. I want you to know that I have never paid a debt more willingly."

When all was done with, and we saw the last of Reece Morley riding away in the custody of the sheriff and Big Wes, and had taken leave of Father's Indian friends, all but Billy Crow, we sat in quiet reflection around the dining table with Ah Sing attending us.

Mr. Logan advised me to use my monies for the schooling he and Father agreed was right for me. The law, Mr. Logan thought from his own experience and ours, was the most-needed profession for our vast and growing country.

Though few knew better than I the need of an honest man of law in Solace, I could not see myself sitting over a desk in a closed-in room, shut away from the high mountain meadows, the singing winds and the rivers that I loved so well. No money could buy this for me, and I firmly said so. I would go to school and I would study law for its usefulness, but then I would return to Solace and the Deakens land to live as had my grandfather and Father. Hadn't Grandfather served the country well in both his callings; and Father, too, who had forsaken teaching for the raising of blooded cattle?

And so it was agreed. With the money that was to be mine I could do all the things I had hoped to do, although not so lavishly as if I had found the hidden place of the Indian gold. I could buy for Rachel . . .

Here my thoughts were interrupted by Ah Sing who came shuffling up to the table.

"Indian boy say good-by. He say you go see him first."

"But I thought he was going home with us."

Billy Crow stood waiting before the back door, his bridle

reins over his arm. High on the rim of the canyon trail above the last of the Indian riders was disappearing.

"Aren't you going home with us?" I pleaded, for now more than any other time I wanted the chance to repay all he had done for me. I felt the warmth of kinship for a brother I had never had.

He shook his head in answer. "When snow come, then I come. Now I go with Gray Wolf for the powwow." With that he reached inside his shirt and drew from around his neck a leather thong that held a large and shining nugget of pierced gold. To my amazement, he reached forward and slipped the thong over my head.

Before I could bring myself to speak, he turned about and leaped to his pony and with a dig of his moccasined heels and a lift of the horse's head toward the gate.

"Nika-Mika," he shouted back to me, his dark face bright with laughter.

When I went back inside, sobered at a gift I knew to be the only thing of value Billy Crow possessed, Mr. Logan was still talking.

"If your daughter has a talent for music she must come to us in San Francisco. Study will help her to forget all this."

Father stopped when I asked him for the meaning of Billy Crow's parting words.

"They are the Indian words of binding friendship," he explained. "He is offering you all he has. He is saying 'Nika-Mika, they are yours and mine.'"

It was in this way I came by the present of gold I had first dreamed of giving Rachel. Mr. Logan took it to San Francisco to have it hung on a fine chain and engraved with Billy Crow's words "Nika-Mika."

If, in the time that followed, Holy Joe was disappointed at having to give up our search for the hidden mine, he had little to say about it. When Mr. Logan sold the Lost Creek Ranch to return to San Francisco, Miss Maggie Connell found Joe a more lasting job in Rimrock. As Mrs. Joseph Patrick Brennen, her sharp eyes took the place of his, and her loving care was a thing no gold could have bought.

As for me, I had had enough of adventuring and was well content, as had been Grandfather and Father, to leave to my friends, the Paiutes, their hidden heritage and to return to my own.